No One Writes
to the Colonel
and
Other Stories

*the text of this book is printed
on 100% recycled paper*

No One Writes
to the Colonel

and

Other Stories

GABRIEL GARCÍA MÁRQUEZ
Translated from the Spanish by J. S. Bernstein

HARPER COLOPHON BOOKS
Harper & Row, Publishers
New York, Hagerstown, San Francisco, London

A hardcover edition of this book is published by Harper & Row, Publishers.

"No One Writes to the Colonel" was originally published in Colombia under the title "El Coronel No Tiene Quien Le Escriba," copyright © 1961 by Aguirre Editor, Colombia, South America. "Big Mama's Funeral" was originally published under the title "Los Funerales de la Mama Grande," copyright © 1962 by Universidad Veracruzana, Vera Cruz, Mexico.

First HARPER COLOPHON edition published 1979.

ISBN: 0-06-090700-2

79 80 81 82 83 10 9 8 7 6 5 4 3 2 1

CONTENTS

No One Writes
to the Colonel

THE COLONEL took the top off the coffee can and saw that there was only one little spoonful left. He removed the pot from the fire, poured half the water onto the earthen floor, and scraped the inside of the can with a knife until the last scrapings of the ground coffee, mixed with bits of rust, fell into the pot.

While he was waiting for it to boil, sitting next to the stone fireplace with an attitude of confident and innocent expectation, the colonel experienced the feeling that fungus and poisonous lilies were taking root in his gut. It was October. A difficult morning to get through, even for a man like himself, who had survived so many mornings like this one. For nearly sixty years—since the end of the last civil war—the colonel had done nothing else but wait. October was one of the few things which arrived.

His wife raised the mosquito netting when she saw him come into the bedroom with the coffee. The night before she had suffered an asthma attack, and now she was in a drowsy state. But she sat up to take the cup.

"And you?" she said.

"I've had mine," the colonel lied. "There was still a big spoonful left."

The bells began ringing at that moment. The colonel had forgotten the funeral. While his wife was drinking her coffee, he unhooked the hammock at one end, and rolled it up on the other, behind the door. The woman thought about the dead man.

"He was born in 1922," she said. "Exactly a month after our son. April 7th."

She continued sipping her coffee in the pauses of her grav-

3

elly breathing. She was scarcely more than a bit of white on an arched, rigid spine. Her disturbed breathing made her put her questions as assertions. When she finished her coffee, she was still thinking about the dead man.

"It must be horrible to be buried in October," she said. But her husband paid no attention. He opened the window. October had moved in on the patio. Contemplating the vegetation, which was bursting out in intense greens, and the tiny mounds the worms made in the mud, the colonel felt the sinister month again in his intestines.

"I'm wet through to the bones," he said.

"It's winter," the woman replied. "Since it began raining I've been telling you to sleep with your socks on."

"I've been sleeping with them for a week."

It rained gently but ceaselessly. The colonel would have preferred to wrap himself in a wool blanket and get back into the hammock. But the insistence of the cracked bells reminded him about the funeral. "It's October," he whispered, and walked toward the center of the room. Only then did he remember the rooster tied to the leg of the bed. It was a fighting cock.

After taking the cup into the kitchen, he wound the pendulum clock in its carved wooden case in the living room. Unlike the bedroom, which was too narrow for an asthmatic's breathing, the living room was large, with four sturdy rockers around a little table with a cover and a plaster cat. On the wall opposite the clock, there was a picture of a woman dressed in tulle, surrounded by cupids in a boat laden with roses.

It was seven-twenty when he finished winding the clock. Then he took the rooster into the kitchen, tied it to a leg of the stove, changed the water in the can, and put a handful of corn next to it. A group of children came in through a hole in the fence. They sat around the rooster, to watch it in silence.

"Stop looking at that animal," said the colonel. "Roosters wear out if you look at them so much."

The children didn't move. One of them began playing the chords of a popular song on his harmonica. "Don't play that today," the colonel told him. "There's been a death in town." The child put the instrument in his pants pocket, and the colonel went into the bedroom to dress for the funeral.

Because of his wife's asthma, his white suit was not pressed. So he had to wear the old black suit which since his marriage he used only on special occasions. It took some effort to find it in the bottom of the trunk, wrapped in newspapers and protected against moths with little balls of naphthalene. Stretched out in bed, the woman was still thinking about the dead man.

"He must have met Agustín already," she said. "Maybe he won't tell him about the situation we've been left in since his death."

"At this moment they're probably talking roosters," said the colonel.

He found an enormous old umbrella in the trunk. His wife had won it in a raffle held to collect funds for the colonel's party. That same night they had attended an outdoor show which was not interrupted despite the rain. The colonel, his wife, and their son, Agustín—who was then eight—watched the show until the end, seated under the umbrella. Now Agustín was dead, and the bright satin material had been eaten away by the moths.

"Look what's left of our circus clown's umbrella," said the colonel with one of his old phrases. Above his head a mysterious system of little metal rods opened. "The only thing it's good for now is to count the stars."

He smiled. But the woman didn't take the trouble to look at the umbrella. "Everything's that way," she whispered. "We're rotting alive." And she closed her eyes so she could concentrate on the dead man.

After shaving himself by touch—since he'd lacked a mirror for a long time—the colonel dressed silently. His trousers, almost as tight on his legs as long underwear, closed at the ankles with slip-knotted drawstrings, were held up at the waist by two straps of the same material which passed through two gilt buckles sewn on at kidney height. He didn't use a belt. His shirt, the color of old Manila paper, and as stiff, fastened with a copper stud which served at the same time to hold the detachable collar. But the detachable collar was torn, so the colonel gave up on the idea of a tie.

He did each thing as if it were a transcendent act. The bones in his hands were covered by taut, translucent skin, with light spots like the skin on his neck. Before he put on his patent-leather shoes, he scraped the dried mud from the stitching. His wife saw him at that moment, dressed as he was on their wedding day. Only then did she notice how much her husband had aged.

"You look as if you're dressed for some special event," she said.

"This burial is a special event," the colonel said. "It's the first death from natural causes which we've had in many years."

The weather cleared up after nine. The colonel was getting ready to go out when his wife seized him by the sleeve of his coat.

"Comb your hair," she said.

He tried to subdue his steel-colored, bristly hair with a bone comb. But it was a useless attempt.

"I must look like a parrot," he said.

The woman examined him. She thought he didn't. The

colonel didn't look like a parrot. He was a dry man, with solid bones articulated as if with nuts and bolts. Because of the vitality in his eyes, it didn't seem as if he were preserved in formalin.

"You're fine that way," she admitted, and added, when her husband was leaving the room: "Ask the doctor if we poured boiling water on him in this house."

They lived at the edge of town, in a house with a palm-thatched roof and walls whose whitewash was flaking off. The humidity kept up but the rain had stopped. The colonel went down toward the plaza along an alley with houses crowded in on each other. As he came out into the main street, he shivered. As far as the eye could see, the town was carpeted with flowers. Seated in their doorways, the women in black were waiting for the funeral.

In the plaza it began to drizzle again. The proprietor of the pool hall saw the colonel from the door of his place and shouted to him with open arms:

"Colonel, wait, and I'll lend you an umbrella!"

The colonel replied without turning around.

"Thank you. I'm all right this way."

The funeral procession hadn't come out of church yet. The men—dressed in white with black ties—were talking in the low doorway under their umbrellas. One of them saw the colonel jumping between the puddles in the plaza.

"Get under here, friend!" he shouted.

He made room under the umbrella.

"Thanks, friend," said the colonel.

But he didn't accept the invitation. He entered the house directly to give his condolences to the mother of the dead man. The first thing he perceived was the odor of many different flowers. Then the heat rose. The colonel tried to make his way through the crowd which was jammed into the bedroom. But someone put a hand on his back, pushed him toward the back of the room through a gallery of perplexed faces to the spot where—deep and wide open—the nostrils of the dead man were found.

There was the dead man's mother, shooing the flies away from the coffin with a plaited palm fan. Other women, dressed in black, contemplated the body with the same expression with which one watches the current of a river. All at once a voice started up at the back of the room. The colonel put one woman aside, faced the profile of the dead man's mother, and put a hand on her shoulder.

"I'm so sorry," he said.

She didn't turn her head. She opened her mouth and let out a howl. The colonel started. He felt himself being pushed against the corpse by a shapeless crowd which broke out in a quavering outcry. He looked for a firm support for his hands but couldn't find the wall. There were other bodies in its place. Someone said in his ear, slowly, with a very gentle voice, "Careful, Colonel." He spun his head around and was face to face with the dead man. But he didn't recognize him because he was stiff and dynamic and seemed as disconcerted as he, wrapped in white cloths and with his trumpet in his hands. When the colonel raised his head over the shouts, in search of air, he saw the closed box bouncing toward the door down a slope of flowers which disintegrated against the walls. He perspired. His joints ached. A moment later he knew he was in the street because the drizzle hurt his eyelids, and someone seized him by the arm and said:

"Hurry up, friend, I was waiting for you."

It was Sabas, the godfather of his dead son, the only leader of his party who had escaped political persecution and had continued to live in town. "Thanks, friend," said the colonel, and walked in silence under the umbrella. The band struck up the funeral march. The colonel noticed the lack of a trumpet, and for the first time was certain that the dead man was dead.

"Poor man," he murmured.

Sabas cleared his throat. He held the umbrella in his left hand, the handle almost at the level of his head, since he was shorter than the colonel. They began to talk when the cortege left the plaza. Sabas turned toward the colonel then, his face disconsolate, and said:

"Friend, what's new with the rooster?"

"He's still there," the colonel replied.

At that moment a shout was heard:

"Where are they going with that dead man?"

The colonel raised his eyes. He saw the Mayor on the balcony of the barracks in an expansive pose. He was dressed in his flannel underwear; his unshaven cheek was swollen. The musicians stopped the march. A moment later the colonel recognized Father Angel's voice shouting at the Mayor. He made out their dialogue through the drumming of the rain on the umbrella.

"Well?" asked Sabas.

"Well nothing," the colonel replied. "The burial may not pass in front of the police barracks."

"I had forgotten," exclaimed Sabas. "I always forget that we are under martial law."

"But this isn't a rebellion," the colonel said. "It's a poor dead musician."

The cortege changed direction. In the poor neighborhoods the women watched it pass, biting their nails in silence. But then they came out into the middle of the street and sent up shouts of praise, gratitude, and farewell, as if they believed the dead man was listening to them inside the coffin. The colonel felt ill at the cemetery. When Sabas pushed him toward the wall to make way for the men who were carrying the dead man, he turned his smiling face toward him, but met a rigid countenance.

"What's the matter, friend?" Sabas asked.

The colonel sighed.

"It's October."

They returned by the same street. It had cleared. The sky was deep, intensely blue. It won't rain any more, thought the colonel, and he felt better, but he was still dejected. Sabas interrupted his thoughts.

"Have a doctor examine you."

"I'm not sick," the colonel said. "The trouble is that in October I feel as if I had animals in my gut."

Sabas went "Ah." He said goodbye at the door to his house, a new building, two stories high, with wrought-iron window gratings. The colonel headed for his home, anxious to take off his dress suit. He went out again a moment later to the store on the corner to buy a can of coffee and half a pound of corn for the rooster.

The colonel attended to the rooster in spite of the fact that on Thursday he would have preferred to stay in his hammock. It didn't clear for several days. During the course of the week, the flora in his belly blossomed. He spent several sleepless nights, tormented by the whistling of the asthmatic woman's lungs. But October granted a truce on Friday afternoon. Agustín's companions—workers from the tailor shop, as he had been, and cockfight fanatics—took advantage of the occasion to examine the rooster. He was in good shape.

The colonel returned to the bedroom when he was left alone in the house with his wife. She had recovered.

"What do they say?" she asked.

"Very enthusiastic," the colonel informed her. "Everyone is saving their money to bet on the rooster."

"I don't know what they see in such an ugly rooster," the woman said. "He looks like a freak to me; his head is too tiny for his feet."

"They say he's the best in the district," the colonel answered. "He's worth about fifty pesos."

He was sure that this argument justified his determination to keep the rooster, a legacy from their son who was shot down nine months before at the cockfights for distributing clandestine literature. "An expensive illusion," the woman said. "When the corn is gone we'll have to feed him on our own livers." The colonel took a good long time to think, while he was looking for his white ducks in the closet.

"It's just for a few months," he said. "We already know that there will be fights in January. Then we can sell him for more."

The pants needed pressing. The woman stretched them out over the stove with two irons heated over the coals.

"What's your hurry to go out?" she asked.

"The mail."

"I had forgotten that today is Friday," she commented, returning to the bedroom. The colonel was dressed but pantsless. She observed his shoes.

"Those shoes are ready to throw out," she said. "Keep wearing your patent-leather ones."

The colonel felt desolate.

"They look like the shoes of an orphan," he protested. "Every time I put them on I feel like a fugitive from an asylum."

"We are the orphans of our son," the woman said.

This time, too, she persuaded him. The colonel walked toward the harbor before the whistles of the launches blew. Patent-leather shoes, beltless white ducks, and the shirt without the detachable collar, closed at the neck with the copper stud. He observed the docking of the launches from the shop of Moses the Syrian. The travelers got off, stiff from eight hours of immobility. The same ones as always: traveling salesmen, and people from the town who had left the preceding week and were returning as usual.

The last one was the mail launch. The colonel saw it dock

with an anguished uneasiness. On the roof, tied to the boat's smokestacks and protected by an oilcloth, he spied the mailbag. Fifteen years of waiting had sharpened his intuition. The rooster had sharpened his anxiety. From the moment the postmaster went on board the launch, untied the bag, and hoisted it up on his shoulder, the colonel kept him in sight.

He followed him through the street parallel to the harbor, a labyrinth of stores and booths with colored merchandise on display. Every time he did it, the colonel experienced an anxiety very different from, but just as oppressive as, fright. The doctor was waiting for the newspapers in the post office.

"My wife wants me to ask you if we threw boiling water on you at our house," the colonel said.

He was a young physician with his skull covered by sleek black hair. There was something unbelievable in the perfection of his dentition. He asked after the health of the asthmatic. The colonel supplied a detailed report without taking his eyes off the postmaster, who was distributing the letters into cubbyholes. His indolent way of moving exasperated the colonel.

The doctor received his mail with the packet of newspapers. He put the pamphlets of medical advertising to one side. Then he scanned his personal letters. Meanwhile the postmaster was handing out mail to those who were present. The colonel watched the compartment which corresponded to his letter in the alphabet. An air-mail letter with blue borders increased his nervous tension.

The doctor broke the seal on the newspapers. He read the lead items while the colonel—his eyes fixed on the little box—waited for the postmaster to stop in front of it. But he didn't. The doctor interrupted his reading of the newspapers. He looked at the colonel. Then he looked at the postmaster seated in front of the telegraph key, and then again at the colonel.

"We're leaving," he said.

The postmaster didn't raise his head.

"Nothing for the colonel," he said.

The colonel felt ashamed.

"I wasn't expecting anything," he lied. He turned to the doctor with an entirely childish look. "No one writes to me."

They went back in silence. The doctor was concentrating on the newspapers. The colonel with his habitual way of walking which resembled that of a man retracing his steps to look for a lost coin. It was a bright afternoon. The almond trees in the plaza were shedding their last rotted leaves. It had begun to grow dark when they arrived at the door of the doctor's office.

"What's in the news?" the colonel asked.

The doctor gave him a few newspapers.

"No one knows," he said. "It's hard to read between the lines which the censor lets them print."

The colonel read the main headlines. International news. At the top, across four columns, a report on the Suez Canal. The front page was almost completely covered by paid funeral announcements.

"There's no hope of elections," the colonel said.

"Don't be naïve, Colonel," said the doctor. "We're too old now to be waiting for the Messiah."

The colonel tried to give the newspapers back, but the doctor refused them.

"Take them home with you," he said. "You can read them tonight and return them tomorrow."

A little after seven the bells in the tower rang out the censor's movie classifications. Father Angel used this means to announce the moral classification of the film in accordance with the ratings he received every month by mail. The colonel's wife counted twelve bells.

"Unfit for everyone," she said. "It's been about a year now that the movies are bad for everyone."

She lowered the mosquito netting and murmured, "The world is corrupt." But the colonel made no comment. Before lying down, he tied the rooster to the leg of the bed. He locked the house and sprayed some insecticide in the bedroom. Then he put the lamp on the floor, hung his hammock up, and lay down to read the newspapers.

He read them in chronological order, from the first page to the last, including the advertisements. At eleven the trumpet blew curfew. The colonel finished his reading a half-hour later, opened the patio door on the impenetrable night, and urinated, besieged by mosquitoes, against the wall studs. His wife was awake when he returned to the bedroom.

"Nothing about the veterans?" she asked.

"Nothing," said the colonel. He put out the lamp before he got into the hammock. "In the beginning at least they published the list of the new pensioners. But it's been about five years since they've said anything."

It rained after midnight. The colonel managed to get to sleep but woke up a moment later, alarmed by his intestines. He discovered a leak in some part of the roof. Wrapped in a wool blanket up to his ears, he tried to find the leak in the darkness. A trickle of cold sweat slipped down his spine. He had a fever. He felt as if he were floating in concentric circles inside a tank of jelly. Someone spoke. The colonel answered from his revolutionist's cot.

"Who are you talking to?" asked his wife.

"The Englishman disguised as a tiger who appeared at Colonel Aureliano Buendía's camp," the colonel answered. He turned over in his hammock, burning with his fever. "It was the Duke of Marlborough."

The sky was clear at dawn. At the second call for Mass, he jumped from the hammock and installed himself in a confused reality which was agitated by the crowing of the rooster. His head was still spinning in concentric circles. He was nauseous. He went out into the patio and headed for the privy through the barely audible whispers and the dark odors of

winter. The inside of the little zinc-roofed wooden compartment was rarefied by the ammonia smell from the privy. When
the colonel raised the lid, a triangular cloud of flies rushed out
of the pit.

It was a false alarm. Squatting on the platform of unsanded
boards, he felt the uneasiness of an urge frustrated. The op-
pressiveness was substituted by a dull ache in his digestive
tract. "There's no doubt," he murmured. "It's the same every
October." And again he assumed his posture of confident and
innocent expectation until the fungus in his innards was paci-
fied. Then he returned to the bedroom for the rooster.

"Last night you were delirious from fever," his wife said.

She had begun to straighten up the room, having recovered
from a week-long attack. The colonel made an effort to remember.

"It wasn't fever," he lied. "It was the dream about the
spider webs again."

As always happened, the woman emerged from her attack full
of nervous energy. In the course of the morning she turned the
house upside down. She changed the position of everything,
except the clock and the picture of the young girl. She was so
thin and sinewy that when she walked about in her cloth slippers and her black dress all buttoned up she seemed as if
she had the power of walking through the walls. But before
twelve she had regained her bulk, her human weight. In bed
she was an empty space. Now, moving among the flowerpots
of ferns and begonias, her presence overflowed the house. "If
Agustín's year were up, I would start singing," she said
while she stirred the pot where all the things to eat that the
tropical land is capable of producing, cut into pieces, were
boiling.

"If you feel like singing, sing," said the colonel. "It's good
for your spleen."

The doctor came after lunch. The colonel and his wife were

drinking coffee in the kitchen when he pushed open the street door and shouted:

"Everybody dead?"

The colonel got up to welcome him.

"So it seems, Doctor," he said, going into the living room. "I've always said that your clock keeps time with the buzzards."

The woman went into the bedroom to get ready for the examination. The doctor stayed in the living room with the colonel. In spite of the heat, his immaculate linen suit gave off a smell of freshness. When the woman announced that she was ready, the doctor gave the colonel three sheets of paper in an envelope. He entered the bedroom, saying, "That's what the newspapers didn't print yesterday."

The colonel had assumed as much. It was a summary of the events in the country, mimeographed for clandestine circulation. Revelations about the state of armed resistance in the interior of the country. He felt defeated. Ten years of clandestine reports had not taught him that no news was more surprising than next month's news. He had finished reading when the doctor came back into the living room.

"This patient is healthier than I am," he said. "With asthma like that, I could live to be a hundred."

The colonel glowered at him. He gave him back the envelope without saying a word, but the doctor refused to take it.

"Pass it on," he said in a whisper.

The colonel put the envelope in his pants pocket. The woman came out of the bedroom, saying, "One of these days I'll up and die, and carry you with me, off to hell, Doctor." The doctor responded silently with the stereotyped enamel of his teeth. He pulled a chair up to the little table and took several jars of free samples out of his bag. The woman went on into the kitchen.

"Wait and I'll warm up the coffee."

"No, thank you very much," said the doctor. He wrote the

proper dosage on a prescription pad. "I absolutely refuse to give you the chance to poison me."

She laughed in the kitchen. When he finished writing, the doctor read the prescription aloud, because he knew that no one could decipher his handwriting. The colonel tried to concentrate. Returning from the kitchen, the woman discovered in his face the toll of the previous night.

"This morning he had a fever," she said, pointing at her husband. "He spent about two hours talking nonsense about the civil war."

The colonel started.

"It wasn't a fever," he insisted, regaining his composure. "Furthermore," he said, "the day I feel sick I'll throw myself into the garbage can on my own."

He went into the bedroom to find the newspapers.

"Thank you for the compliment," the doctor said.

They walked together toward the plaza. The air was dry. The tar on the streets had begun to melt from the heat. When the doctor said goodbye, the colonel asked him in a low voice, his teeth clenched:

"How much do we owe you, Doctor?"

"Nothing, for now," the doctor said, and he gave him a pat on the shoulder. "I'll send you a fat bill when the cock wins."

The colonel went to the tailor shop to take the clandestine letter to Agustín's companions. It was his only refuge ever since his co-partisans had been killed or exiled from town and he had been converted into a man with no other occupation than waiting for the mail every Friday.

The afternoon heat stimulated the woman's energy. Seated among the begonias in the veranda next to a box of worn-out clothing, she was again working the eternal miracle of creating new apparel out of nothing. She made collars from sleeves, and cuffs from the backs and square patches, perfect ones, although with scraps of different colors. A cicada lodged its whistle in the patio. The sun faded. But she didn't see it go down over the begonias. She raised her head only at dusk when the colonel returned home. Then she clasped her neck with both hands, cracked her knuckles, and said:

"My head is as stiff as a board."

"It's always been that way," the colonel said, but then he saw his wife's body covered all over with scraps of color. "You look like a magpie."

"One has to be half a magpie to dress you," she said. She held out a shirt made of three different colors of material except for the collar and cuffs, which were the same color. "At the carnival all you have to do is take off your jacket."

The six-o'clock bells interrupted her. "The Angel of the Lord announced unto Mary," she prayed aloud, heading into the bedroom. The colonel talked to the children who had come to look at the rooster after school. Then he remembered that there was no corn for the next day, and entered the bedroom to ask his wife for money.

"I think there's only fifty cents," she said.

She kept the money under the mattress, knotted into the corner of a handkerchief. It was the proceeds of Agustín's sewing machine. For nine months, they had spent that money penny by penny, parceling it out between their needs and the rooster's. Now there were only two twenty-cent pieces and a ten-cent piece left.

"Buy a pound of corn," the woman said. "With the change, buy tomorrow's coffee and four ounces of cheese."

"And a golden elephant to hang in the doorway," the colonel went on. "The corn alone costs forty-two."

They thought a moment. "The rooster is an animal, and therefore he can wait," said the woman at first. But her husband's expression caused her to reflect. The colonel sat on the bed, his elbows on his knees, jingling the coins in his hands. "It's not for my sake," he said after a moment. "If it depended on me I'd make a rooster stew this very evening. A fifty-peso indigestion would be very good." He paused to squash a mosquito on his neck. Then his eyes followed his wife around the room.

"What bothers me is that those poor boys are saving up."

Then she began to think. She turned completely around with the insecticide bomb. The colonel found something unreal in her attitude, as if she were invoking the spirits of the house for a consultation. At last she put the bomb on the little mantel with the prints on it, and fixed her syrup-colored eyes on the syrup-colored eyes of the colonel.

"Buy the corn," she said. "God knows how we'll manage."

"This is the miracle of the multiplying loaves," the colonel repeated every time they sat down to the table during the following week. With her astonishing capacity for darning, sewing, and mending, she seemed to have discovered the key to sustaining the household economy with no money. October prolonged its truce. The humidity was replaced by sleepiness. Comforted by the copper sun, the woman devoted three afternoons to her complicated hairdo. "High Mass has begun," the colonel said one afternoon when she was getting the knots out of her long blue tresses with a comb which had some teeth missing. The second afternoon, seated in the patio with a white sheet in her lap, she used a finer comb to take out the lice which had proliferated during her attack. Lastly, she washed her hair with lavender water, waited for it to dry, and rolled it up on the nape of her neck in two turns held with a barrette. The colonel waited. At night, sleepless in his hammock, he worried for many hours over the rooster's fate. But on Wednesday they weighed him, and he was in good shape.

That same afternoon, when Agustín's companions left the house counting the imaginary proceeds from the rooster's victory, the colonel also felt in good shape. His wife cut his hair. "You've taken twenty years off me," he said, examining his head with his hands. His wife thought her husband was right.

"When I'm well, I can bring back the dead," she said.

But her conviction lasted for a very few hours. There was no longer anything in the house to sell, except the clock and the picture. Thursday night, at the limit of their resources, the woman showed her anxiety over the situation.

"Don't worry," the colonel consoled her. "The mail comes tomorrow."

The following day he waited for the launches in front of the doctor's office.

"The airplane is a marvelous thing," the colonel said, his eyes resting on the mailbag. "They say you can get to Europe in one night."

"That's right," the doctor said, fanning himself with an illustrated magazine. The colonel spied the postmaster among a group waiting for the docking to end so they could jump onto the launch. The postmaster jumped first. He received from the captain an envelope sealed with wax. Then he climbed up onto the roof. The mailbag was tied between two oil drums.

"But still it has its dangers," said the colonel. He lost the postmaster from sight, but saw him again among the colored bottles on the refreshment cart. "Humanity doesn't progress without paying a price."

"Even at this stage it's safer than a launch," the doctor said. "At twenty thousand feet you fly above the weather."

"Twenty thousand feet," the colonel repeated, perplexed, without being able to imagine what the figure meant.

The doctor became interested. He spread out the magazine with both hands until it was absolutely still.

"There's perfect stability," he said.

But the colonel was hanging on the actions of the postmaster. He saw him consume a frothy pink drink, holding the glass in his left hand. In his right he held the mailbag.

"Also, on the ocean there are ships at anchor in continual

contact with night flights," the doctor went on. "With so many precautions it's safer than a launch."

The colonel looked at him.

"Naturally," he said. "It must be like a carpet."

The postmaster came straight toward them. The colonel stepped back, impelled by an irresistible anxiety, trying to read the name written on the sealed envelope. The postmaster opened the bag. He gave the doctor his packet of newspapers. Then he tore open the envelope with the personal correspondence, checked the correctness of the receipt, and read the addressee's names off the letters. The doctor opened the newspapers.

"Still the problem with Suez," he said, reading the main headlines. "The West is losing ground."

The colonel didn't read the headlines. He made an effort to control his stomach. "Ever since there's been censorship, the newspapers talk only about Europe," he said. "The best thing would be for the Europeans to come over here and for us to go to Europe. That way everybody would know what's happening in his own country."

"To the Europeans, South America is a man with a mustache, a guitar, and a gun," the doctor said, laughing over his newspaper. "They don't understand the problem."

The postmaster delivered his mail. He put the rest in the bag and closed it again. The doctor got ready to read two personal letters, but before tearing open the envelopes he looked at the colonel. Then he looked at the postmaster.

"Nothing for the colonel?"

The colonel was terrified. The postmaster tossed the bag onto his shoulder, got off the platform, and replied without turning his head:

"No one writes to the colonel."

Contrary to his habit, he didn't go directly home. He had a cup of coffee at the tailor's while Agustín's companions leafed through the newspapers. He felt cheated. He would have preferred to stay there until the next Friday to keep from having to face his wife that night with empty hands. But when the tailor shop closed, he had to face up to reality. His wife was waiting for him.

"Nothing?" she asked.

"Nothing," the colonel answered.

The following Friday he went down to the launches again. And, as on every Friday, he returned home without the longed-for letter. "We've waited long enough," his wife told him that night. "One must have the patience of an ox, as you do, to wait for a letter for fifteen years." The colonel got into his hammock to read the newspapers.

"We have to wait our turn," he said. "Our number is 1823."

"Since we've been waiting, that number has come up twice in the lottery," his wife replied.

The colonel read, as usual, from the first page to the last, including the advertisements. But this time he didn't concentrate. During his reading, he thought about his veteran's pension. Nineteen years before, when Congress passed the law, it took him eight years to prove his claim. Then it took him six more years to get himself included on the rolls. That was the last letter the colonel had received.

He finished after curfew sounded. When he went to turn off the lamp, he realized that his wife was awake.

"Do you still have that clipping?"

The woman thought.

"Yes. It must be with the other papers."

She got out of her mosquito netting and took a wooden chest out of the closet, with a packet of letters arranged by date and held together by a rubber band. She located the advertisement of a law firm which promised quick action on war pensions.

"We could have spent the money in the time I've wasted

trying to convince you to change lawyers," the woman said, handing her husband the newspaper clipping. "We're not getting anything out of their putting us away on a shelf as they do with the Indians."

The colonel read the clipping dated two years before. He put it in the pocket of his jacket which was hanging behind the door.

"The problem is that to change lawyers you need money."

"Not at all," the woman said decisively. "You write them telling them to discount whatever they want from the pension itself when they collect it. It's the only way they'll take the case."

So Saturday afternoon the colonel went to see his lawyer. He found him stretched out lazily in a hammock. He was a monumental Negro, with nothing but two canines in his upper jaw. The lawyer put his feet into a pair of wooden-soled slippers and opened the office window on a dusty pianola with papers stuffed into the compartments where the rolls used to go: clippings from the *Official Gazette*, pasted into old accounting ledgers, and a jumbled collection of accounting bulletins. The keyless pianola did double duty as a desk. The lawyer sat down in a swivel chair. The colonel expressed his uneasiness before revealing the purpose of his visit.

"I warned you that it would take more than a few days," said the lawyer when the colonel paused. He was sweltering in the heat. He adjusted the chair backward and fanned himself with an advertising brochure.

"My agents write to me frequently, saying not to get impatient."

"It's been that way for fifteen years," the colonel answered. "This is beginning to sound like the story about the capon."

The lawyer gave a very graphic description of the administrative ins and outs. The chair was too narrow for his sagging buttocks. "Fifteen years ago it was easier," he said.

"Then there was the city's veterans' organization, with members of both parties." His lungs filled with stifling air and he pronounced the sentence as if he had just invented it:

"There's strength in numbers."

"There wasn't in this case," the colonel said, realizing his aloneness for the first time. "All my comrades died waiting for the mail."

The lawyer didn't change his expression.

"The law was passed too late," he said. "Not everybody was as lucky as you to be a colonel at the age of twenty. Furthermore, no special allocation was included, so the government has had to make adjustments in the budget."

Always the same story. Each time the colonel listened to him, he felt a mute resentment. "This is not charity," he said. "It's not a question of doing us a favor. We broke our backs to save the Republic." The lawyer threw up his hands.

"That's the way it is," he said. "Human ingratitude knows no limits."

The colonel also knew that story. He had begun hearing it the day after the Treaty of Neerlandia, when the government promised travel assistance and indemnities to two hundred revolutionary officers. Camped at the base of the gigantic silk-cotton tree at Neerlandia, a revolutionary battalion, made up in great measure of youths who had left school, waited for three months. Then they went back to their homes by their own means, and they kept on waiting there. Almost sixty years later, the colonel was still waiting.

Excited by these memories, he adopted a transcendental attitude. He rested his right hand on his thigh—mere bone sewed together with nerve tissue—and murmured:

"Well, I've decided to take action."

The lawyer waited.

"Such as?"

"To change lawyers."

A mother duck, followed by several little ducklings, entered the office. The lawyer sat up to chase them out. "As you wish, Colonel," he said, chasing the animals. "It will be just as you wish. If I could work miracles, I wouldn't be living in this barnyard." He put a wooden grille across the patio door and returned to his chair.

"My son worked all his life," said the colonel. "My house is mortgaged. That retirement law has been a lifetime pension for lawyers."

"Not for me," the lawyer protested. "Every last cent has gone for my expenses."

The colonel suffered at the thought that he had been unjust.

"That's what I meant," he corrected himself. He dried his forehead with the sleeve of his shirt. "This heat is enough to rust the screws in your head."

A moment later the lawyer was turning the office upside down looking for the power of attorney. The sun advanced toward the center of the tiny room, which was built of unsanded boards. After looking futilely everywhere, the lawyer got down on all fours, huffing and puffing, and picked up a roll of papers from under the pianola.

"Here it is."

He gave the colonel a sheet of paper with a seal on it. "I have to write my agents so they can cancel the copies," he concluded. The colonel shook the dust off the paper and put it in his shirt pocket.

"Tear it up yourself," the lawyer said.

"No," the colonel answered. "These are twenty years of memories." And he waited for the lawyer to keep on looking. But the lawyer didn't. He went to the hammock to wipe off his sweat. From there he looked at the colonel through the shimmering air.

"I need the documents also," the colonel said.

"Which ones?"

"The proof of claim."

The lawyer threw up his hands.

"Now, that would be impossible, Colonel."

The colonel became alarmed. As Treasurer of the revolution in the district of Macondo, he had undertaken a difficult six-day journey with the funds for the civil war in two trunks roped to the back of a mule. He arrived at the camp of Neerlandia dragging the mule, which was dead from hunger, half an hour before the treaty was signed. Colonel Aureliano Buendía—quartermaster general of the revolutionary forces on the Atlantic coast—held out the receipt for the funds, and included the two trunks in his inventory of the surrender.

"Those documents have an incalculable value," the colonel said. "There's a receipt from Colonel Aureliano Buendía, written in his own hand."

"I agree," said the lawyer. "But those documents have passed through thousands and thousands of hands, in thousands and thousands of offices, before they reached God knows which department in the War Ministry."

"No official could fail to notice documents like those," the colonel said.

"But the officials have changed many times in the last fifteen years," the lawyer pointed out. "Just think about it; there have been seven Presidents, and each President changed his Cabinet at least ten times, and each Minister changed his staff at least a hundred times."

"But nobody could take the documents home," said the colonel. "Each new official must have found them in the proper file."

The lawyer lost his patience.

"And moreover if those papers are removed from the Ministry now, they will have to wait for a new place on the rolls."

"It doesn't matter," the colonel said.

"It'll take centuries."

"It doesn't matter. If you wait for the big things, you can wait for the little ones."

He took a pad of lined paper, the pen, the inkwell, and a blotter to the little table in the living room, and left the bedroom door open in case he had to ask his wife anything. She was saying her beads.

"What's today's date?"

"October 27th."

He wrote with a studious neatness, the hand that held the pen resting on the blotter, his spine straight to ease his breathing, as he'd been taught in school. The heat became unbearable in the closed living room. A drop of perspiration fell on the letter. The colonel picked it up on the blotter. Then he tried to erase the letters which had smeared but he smudged them. He didn't lose his patience. He wrote an asterisk and noted in the margin, "acquired rights." Then he read the whole paragraph.

"When was I put on the rolls?"

The woman didn't interrupt her prayer to think.

"August 12, 1949."

A moment later it began to rain. The colonel filled a page with large doodlings which were a little childish, the same ones he learned in public school at Manaure. Then he wrote on a second sheet down to the middle, and he signed it.

He read the letter to his wife. She approved each sentence with a nod. When he finished reading, the colonel sealed the envelope and turned off the lamp.

"You could ask someone to type it for you."

"No," the colonel answered. "I'm tired of going around asking favors."

For half an hour he heard the rain against the palm roof. The town sank into the deluge. After curfew sounded, a leak began somewhere in the house.

"This should have been done a long time ago," the woman said. "It's always better to handle things oneself."

"It's never too late," the colonel said, paying attention to the leak. "Maybe all this will be settled when the mortgage on the house falls due."

"In two years," the woman said.

He lit the lamp to locate the leak in the living room. He put the rooster's can underneath it and returned to the bedroom, pursued by the metallic noise of the water in the empty can.

"It's possible that to save the interest on the money they'll settle it before January," he said, and he convinced himself. "By then, Agustín's year will be up and we can go to the movies."

She laughed under her breath. "I don't even remember the cartoons any more," she said. The colonel tried to look at her through the mosquito netting.

"When did you go to the movies last?"

"In 1931," she said. "They were showing *The Dead Man's Will.*"

"Was there a fight?"

"We never found out. The storm broke just when the ghost tried to rob the girl's necklace."

The sound of the rain put them to sleep. The colonel felt a slight queasiness in his intestines. But he wasn't afraid. He was about to survive another October. He wrapped himself in a wool blanket, and for a moment heard the gravelly breathing of his wife—far away—drifting on another dream. Then he spoke, completely conscious.

The woman woke up.

"Who are you speaking to?"

"No one," the colonel said. "I was thinking that at the Macondo meeting we were right when we told Colonel Aureliano Buendía not to surrender. That's what started to ruin everything."

It rained the whole week. The second of November—against the colonel's wishes—the woman took flowers to Agustín's grave. She returned from the cemetery and had another attack. It was a hard week. Harder than the four weeks of October which the colonel hadn't thought he'd survive. The doctor came to see the sick woman, and came out of the room shouting, "With asthma like that, I'd be able to bury the whole town!" But he spoke to the colonel alone and prescribed a special diet.

The colonel also suffered a relapse. He strained for many hours in the privy, in an icy sweat, feeling as if he were rotting and that the flora in his vitals was falling to pieces. "It's winter," he repeated to himself patiently. "Everything will be different when it stops raining." And he really believed it, certain that he would be alive at the moment the letter arrived.

This time it was he who had to repair their household economy. He had to grit his teeth many times to ask for credit in the neighborhood stores. "It's just until next week," he would say, without being sure himself that it was true. "It's a little money which should have arrived last Friday." When her attack was over, the woman examined him in horror.

"You're nothing but skin and bones," she said.

"I'm taking care of myself so I can sell myself," the colonel said. "I've already been hired by a clarinet factory."

But in reality his hoping for the letter barely sustained him. Exhausted, his bones aching from sleeplessness, he couldn't attend to his needs and the rooster's at the same time. In the second half of November, he thought that the animal would die after two days without corn. Then he remembered a handful of beans which he had hung in the chimney in July. He opened the pods and put down a can of dry seeds for the rooster.

"Come here," she said.

"Just a minute," the colonel answered, watching the rooster's reaction. "Beggars can't be choosers."

He found his wife trying to sit up in bed. Her ravaged body gave off the aroma of medicinal herbs. She spoke her words, one by one, with calculated precision:

"Get rid of that rooster right now."

The colonel had foreseen that moment. He had been waiting for it ever since the afternoon when his son was shot down, and he had decided to keep the rooster. He had had time to think.

"It's not worth it now," he said. "The fight will be in two months and then we'll be able to sell him at a better price."

"It's not a question of the money," the woman said. "When the boys come, you'll tell them to take it away and do whatever they feel like with it."

"It's for Agustín," the colonel said, advancing his prepared argument. "Remember his face when he came to tell us the rooster won."

The woman, in fact, did think of her son.

"Those accursed roosters were his downfall!" she shouted. "If he'd stayed home on January 3rd, his evil hour wouldn't have come." She held out a skinny forefinger toward the door and exclaimed:

"It seems as if I can see him when he left with the rooster under his arm. I warned him not to go looking for trouble at the cockfights, and he smiled and told me, 'Shut up; this afternoon we'll be rolling in money.'"

She fell back exhausted. The colonel pushed her gently toward the pillow. His eyes fell upon other eyes exactly like his own. "Try not to move," he said, feeling her whistling within his own lungs. The woman fell into a momentary torpor. She closed her eyes. When she opened them again, her breathing seemed more even.

"It's because of the situation we're in," she said. "It's a sin to take the food out of our mouths to give it to a rooster."

The colonel wiped her forehead with the sheet.

"Nobody dies in three months."

"And what do we eat in the meantime?" the woman asked.

"I don't know," the colonel said. "But if we were going to die of hunger, we would have died already."

The rooster was very much alive next to the empty can. When he saw the colonel, he emitted an almost human, guttural monologue and tossed his head back. He gave him a smile of complicity:

"Life is tough, pal."

The colonel went into the street. He wandered about the town during the siesta, without thinking about anything, without even trying to convince himself that his problem had no solution. He walked through forgotten streets until he found he was exhausted. Then he returned to the house. The woman heard him come in and called him into the bedroom.

"What?"

She replied without looking at him.

"We can sell the clock."

The colonel had thought of that. "I'm sure Alvaro will give you forty pesos right on the spot," said the woman. "Think how quickly he bought the sewing machine."

She was referring to the tailor whom Agustín had worked for.

"I could speak to him in the morning," admitted the colonel.

"None of that 'speak to him in the morning,'" she insisted. "Take the clock to him this minute. You put it on the counter and you tell him, 'Alvaro, I've brought this clock for you to buy from me.' He'll understand immediately."

The colonel felt ashamed.

"It's like walking around with the Holy Sepulcher," he protested. "If they see me in the street with a showpiece like that, Rafael Escalona will put me into one of his songs."

But this time, too, his wife convinced him. She herself took down the clock, wrapped it in newspaper, and put it into his arms. "Don't come back here without the forty pesos," she said. The colonel went off to the tailor's with the package under his arm. He found Agustín's companions sitting in the doorway.

One of them offered him a seat. "Thanks," he said. "I can't stay." Alvaro came out of the shop. A piece of wet duck hung on a wire stretched between two hooks in the hall. He was a boy with a hard, angular body and wild eyes. He also invited him to sit down. The colonel felt comforted. He leaned the stool against the doorjamb and sat down to wait until Alvaro was alone to propose his deal. Suddenly he realized that he was surrounded by expressionless faces.

"I'm not interrupting?" he said.

They said he wasn't. One of them leaned toward him. He said in a barely audible voice:

"Agustín wrote."

The colonel observed the deserted street.

"What does he say?"

"The same as always."

They gave him the clandestine sheet of paper. The colonel put it in his pants pocket. Then he kept silent, drumming on the package, until he realized that someone had noticed it. He stopped in suspense.

"What have you got there, Colonel?"

The colonel avoided Hernán's penetrating green eyes.

"Nothing," he lied. "I'm taking my clock to the German to have him fix it for me."

"Don't be silly, Colonel," said Hernán, trying to take the package. "Wait and I'll look at it."

The colonel held back. He didn't say anything, but his eyelids turned purple. The others insisted.

"Let him, Colonel. He knows mechanical things."

"I just don't want to bother him."

"Bother, it's no bother," Hernán argued. He seized the clock. "The German will get ten pesos out of you and it'll be the same as it is now."

Hernán went into the tailor shop with the clock. Alvaro was sewing on a machine. At the back, beneath a guitar hanging on a nail, a girl was sewing buttons on. There was a sign tacked up over the guitar: "TALKING POLITICS FORBIDDEN." Outside, the colonel felt as if his body were superfluous. He rested his feet on the rail of the stool.

"Goddamn it, Colonel."

He was startled. "No need to swear," he said.

Alfonso adjusted his eyeglasses on his nose to examine the colonel's shoes.

"It's because of your shoes," he said. "You've got on some goddamn new shoes."

"But you can say that without swearing," the colonel said, and showed the soles of his patent-leather shoes. "These monstrosities are forty years old, and it's the first time they've ever heard anyone swear."

"All done," shouted Hernán, inside, just as the clock's bell rang. In the neighboring house, a woman pounded on the partition; she shouted:

"Let that guitar alone! Agustín's year isn't up yet."

Someone guffawed.

"It's a clock."

Hernán came out with the package.

"It wasn't anything," he said. "If you like I'll go home with you to level it."

The colonel refused his offer.

"How much do I owe you?"

"Don't worry about it, Colonel," replied Hernán, taking his

place in the group. "In January, the rooster will pay for it."

The colonel now found the chance he was looking for.

"I'll make you a deal," he said.

"What?"

"I'll give you the rooster." He examined the circle of faces. "I'll give the rooster to all of you."

Hernán looked at him in confusion.

"I'm too old now for that," the colonel continued. He gave his voice a convincing severity. "It's too much responsibility for me. For days now I've had the impression that the animal is dying."

"Don't worry about it, Colonel," Alfonso said. "The trouble is that the rooster is molting now. He's got a fever in his quills."

"He'll be better next month," Hernán said.

"I don't want him anyway," the colonel said.

Hernán's pupils bore into his.

"Realize how things are, Colonel," he insisted. "The main thing is for you to be the one who puts Agustín's rooster into the ring."

The colonel thought about it. "I realize," he said. "That's why I've kept him until now." He clenched his teeth, and felt he could go on:

"The trouble is there are still two months."

Hernán was the one who understood.

"If it's only because of that, there's no problem," he said.

And he proposed his formula. The other accepted. At dusk, when he entered the house with the package under his arm, his wife was chagrined.

"Nothing?" she asked.

"Nothing," the colonel answered. "But now it doesn't matter. The boys will take over feeding the rooster."

"Wait and I'll lend you an umbrella, friend."

Sabas opened a cupboard in the office wall. He uncovered a jumbled interior: riding boots piled up, stirrups and reins, and an aluminum pail full of riding spurs. Hanging from the upper part, half a dozen umbrellas and a lady's parasol. The colonel was thinking of the debris from some catastrophe.

"Thanks, friend," the colonel said, leaning on the window. "I prefer to wait for it to clear." Sabas didn't close the cupboard. He settled down at the desk within range of the electric fan. Then he took a little hypodermic syringe wrapped in cotton out of the drawer. The colonel observed the grayish almond trees through the rain. It was an empty afternoon.

"The rain is different from this window," he said. "It's as if it were raining in another town."

"Rain is rain from whatever point," replied Sabas. He put the syringe on to boil on the glass desk top. "This town stinks."

The colonel shrugged his shoulders. He walked toward the middle of the office: a green-tiled room with furniture upholstered in brightly colored fabrics. At the back, piled up in disarray, were sacks of salt, honeycombs, and riding saddles. Sabas followed him with a completely vacant stare.

"If I were in your shoes I wouldn't think that way," said the colonel.

He sat down and crossed his legs, his calm gaze fixed on the man leaning over his desk. A small man, corpulent, but with flaccid flesh, he had the sadness of a toad in his eyes.

"Have the doctor look at you, friend," said Sabas. "You've been a little sad since the day of the funeral."

The colonel raised his head.

"I'm perfectly well," he said.

Sabas waited for the syringe to boil. "I wish I could say the same," he complained. "You're lucky because you've got a cast-iron stomach." He contemplated the hairy backs of his hands which were dotted with dark blotches. He wore a ring with a black stone next to his wedding band.

"That's right," the colonel admitted.

Sabas called his wife through the door between the office and the rest of the house. Then he began a painful explanation of his diet. He took a little bottle out of his shirt pocket and put a white pill the size of a pea on the desk.

"It's torture to go around with this everyplace," he said. "It's like carrying death in your pocket."

The colonel approached the desk. He examined the pill in the palm of his hand until Sabas invited him to taste it.

"It's to sweeten coffee," he explained. "It's sugar, but without sugar."

"Of course," the colonel said, his saliva impregnated with a sad sweetness. "It's something like a ringing but without bells."

Sabas put his elbows on the desk with his face in his hands after his wife gave him the injection. The colonel didn't know what to do with his body. The woman unplugged the electric fan, put it on top of the safe, and then went to the cupboard.

"Umbrellas have something to do with death," she said.

The colonel paid no attention to her. He had left his house at four to wait for the mail, but the rain made him take refuge in Sabas's office. It was still raining when the launches whistled.

"Everybody says death is a woman," the woman continued. She was fat, taller than her husband, and had a hairy mole on her upper lip. Her way of speaking reminded one of the hum of the electric fan. "But I don't think it's a woman," she said. She closed the cupboard and looked into the colonel's eyes again.

"I think it's an animal with claws."

"That's possible," the colonel admitted. "At times very strange things happen."

He thought of the postmaster jumping onto the launch in an oilskin slicker. A month had passed since he had changed lawyers. He was entitled to expect a reply. Sabas's wife kept speaking about death until she noticed the colonel's absent-minded expression.

"Friend," she said. "You must be worried."

The colonel sat up.

"That's right, friend," he lied. "I'm thinking that it's five already and the rooster hasn't had his injection."

She was confused.

"An injection for a rooster, as if he were a human being!" she shouted. "That's a sacrilege."

Sabas couldn't stand any more. He raised his flushed face.

"Close your mouth for a minute," he ordered his wife. And in fact she did raise her hands to her mouth. "You've been bothering my friend for half an hour with your foolishness."

"Not at all," the colonel protested.

The woman slammed the door. Sabas dried his neck with a handkerchief soaked in lavender. The colonel approached the window. It was raining steadily. A long-legged chicken was crossing the deserted plaza.

"Is it true the rooster's getting injections?"

"True," said the colonel. "His training begins next week."

"That's madness," said Sabas. "Those things are not for you."

"I agree," said the colonel. "But that's no reason to wring his neck."

"That's just idiotic stubbornness," said Sabas, turning toward the window. The colonel heard him sigh with the breath of a bellows. His friend's eyes made him feel pity.

"It's never too late for anything," the colonel said.

"Don't be unreasonable," insisted Sabas. "It's a two-edged deal. On one side you get rid of that headache, and on the other you can put nine hundred pesos in your pocket."

"Nine hundred pesos!" the colonel exclaimed.

"Nine hundred pesos."

The colonel visualized the figure.

"You think they'd give a fortune like that for the rooster?"

"I don't think," Sabas answered. "I'm absolutely sure."

It was the largest sum the colonel had had in his head since he had returned the revolution's funds. When he left Sabas's office, he felt a strong wrenching in his gut, but he was aware that this time it wasn't because of the weather. At the post office he headed straight for the postmaster:

"I'm expecting an urgent letter," he said. "It's air mail."

The postmaster looked in the cubbyholes. When he finished reading, he put the letters back in the proper box but he didn't say anything. He dusted off his hand and turned a meaningful look on the colonel.

"It was supposed to come today for sure," the colonel said.

The postmaster shrugged.

"The only thing that comes for sure is death, Colonel."

His wife received him with a dish of corn mush. He ate it in silence with long pauses for thought between each spoonful. Seated opposite him, the woman noticed that something had changed in his face.

"What's the matter?" she asked.

"I'm thinking about the employee that pension depends on," the colonel lied. "In fifty years, we'll be peacefully six feet under, while that poor man will be killing himself every Friday waiting for his retirement pension."

"That's a bad sign," the woman said. "It means that you're beginning to resign yourself already." She went on eating her mush. But a moment later she realized that her husband was still far away.

"Now, what you should do is enjoy the mush."

"It's very good," the colonel said. "Where'd it come from?"

"From the rooster," the woman answered. "The boys brought him so much corn that he decided to share it with us. That's life."

"That's right." The colonel sighed. "Life is the best thing that's ever been invented."

He looked at the rooster tied to the leg of the stove and this time he seemed a different animal. The woman also looked at him.

"This afternoon I had to chase the children out with a stick," she said. "They brought an old hen to breed her with the rooster."

"It's not the first time," the colonel said. "That's the same thing they did in those towns with Colonel Aureliano Buendía. They brought him little girls to breed with."

She got a kick out of the joke. The rooster produced a guttural noise which sounded in the hall like quiet human conversation. "Sometimes I think that animal is going to talk," the woman said. The colonel looked at him again.

"He's worth his weight in gold," he said. He made some calculations while he sipped a spoonful of mush. "He'll feed us for three years."

"You can't eat hope," the woman said.

"You can't eat it, but it sustains you," the colonel replied. "It's something like my friend Sabas's miraculous pills."

He slept poorly that night trying to erase the figures from his mind. The following day at lunch, the woman served two plates of mush, and ate hers with her head lowered, without saying a word. The colonel felt himself catching her dark mood.

"What's the matter?"

"Nothing," the woman said.

He had the impression that this time it had been her turn to lie. He tried to comfort her. But the woman persisted.

"It's nothing unusual," she said. "I was thinking that the man has been dead for two months, and I still haven't been to see the family."

So she went to see them that night. The colonel accom-

panied her to the dead man's house, and then headed for the
movie theater, drawn by the music coming over the loud-
speakers. Seated at the door of his office, Father Angel was
watching the entrance to find out who was attending the show
despite his twelve warnings. The flood of light, the strident
music, and the shouts of the children erected a physical resistance in the area. One of the children threatened the colonel with a wooden rifle.

"What's new with the rooster, Colonel?" he said in an
authoritative voice.

The colonel put his hands up.

"He's still around."

A four-color poster covered the entire front of the theater:
Midnight Virgin. She was a woman in an evening gown, with
one leg bared up to the thigh. The colonel continued wandering around the neighborhood until distant thunder and lightning began. Then he went back for his wife.

She wasn't at the dead man's house. Nor at home. The
colonel reckoned that there was little time left before curfew,
but the clock had stopped. He waited, feeling the storm advance on the town. He was getting ready to go out again when
his wife arrived.

He took the rooster into the bedroom. She changed her
clothes and went to take a drink of water in the living room
just as the colonel finished winding the clock, and was waiting
for curfew to blow in order to set it.

"Where were you?" the colonel asked.

"Roundabout," the woman answered. She put the glass on
the washstand without looking at her husband and returned to
the bedroom. "No one thought it was going to rain so soon."
The colonel made no comment. When curfew blew, he set the
clock at eleven, closed the case, and put the chair back in its
place. He found his wife saying her rosary.

"You haven't answered my question," the colonel said.

"What?"

"Where were you?"

"I stayed around there talking," she said. "It had been so long since I'd been out of the house."

The colonel hung up his hammock. He locked the house and fumigated the room. Then he put the lamp on the floor and lay down.

"I understand," he said sadly. "The worst of a bad situation is that it makes us tell lies."

She let out a long sigh.

"I was with Father Angel," she said. "I went to ask him for a loan on our wedding rings."

"And what did he tell you?"

"That it's a sin to barter with sacred things."

She went on talking under her mosquito netting. "Two days ago I tried to sell the clock," she said. "No one is interested because they're selling modern clocks with luminous numbers on the installment plan. You can see the time in the dark." The colonel acknowledged that forty years of shared living, of shared hunger, of shared suffering, had not been enough for him to come to know his wife. He felt that something had also grown old in their love.

"They don't want the picture, either," she said. "Almost everybody has the same one. I even went to the Turk's."

The colonel felt bitter.

"So now everyone knows we're starving."

"I'm tired," the woman said. "Men don't understand problems of the household. Several times I've had to put stones on to boil so the neighbors wouldn't know that we often go for many days without putting on the pot."

The colonel felt offended.

"That's really a humiliation," he said.

The woman got out from under the mosquito netting and went to the hammock. "I'm ready to give up affectation and pretense in this house," she said. Her voice began to darken with rage. "I'm fed up with resignation and dignity."

The colonel didn't move a muscle.

"Twenty years of waiting for the little colored birds which they promised you after every election, and all we've got out of it is a dead son," she went on. "Nothing but a dead son."

The colonel was used to that sort of recrimination.

"We did our duty."

"And they did theirs by making a thousand pesos a month in the Senate for twenty years," the woman answered. "There's my friend Sabas with a two-story house that isn't big enough to keep all his money in, a man who came to this town selling medicines with a snake curled around his neck."

"But he's dying of diabetes," the colonel said.

"And you're dying of hunger," the woman said. "You should realize that you can't eat dignity."

The lightning interrupted her. The thunder exploded in the street, entered the bedroom, and went rolling under the bed like a heap of stones. The woman jumped toward the mosquito netting for her rosary.

The colonel smiled.

"That's what happens to you for not holding your tongue," he said. "I've always said that God is on my side."

But in reality he felt embittered. A moment later he put out the light and sank into thought in a darkness rent by the lightning. He remembered Macondo. The colonel had waited ten years for the promises of Neerlandia to be fulfilled. In the drowsiness of the siesta he saw a yellow, dusty train pull in, with men and women and animals suffocating from the heat, piled up even on the roofs of the cars. It was the banana fever.

In twenty-four hours they had transformed the town. "I'm leaving," the colonel said then. "The odor of the banana is eating at my insides." And he left Macondo on the return train, Wednesday, June 27, 1906, at 2:18 P.M. It took him nearly half a century to realize that he hadn't had a moment's peace since the surrender at Neerlandia.

He opened his eyes.

"Then there's no need to think about it any more," he said.

"What?"

"The problem of the rooster," the colonel said. "Tomorrow I'll sell it to my friend Sabas for nine hundred pesos."

The howls of the castrated animals, fused with Sabas's shouting, came through the office window. If he doesn't come in ten minutes I'll leave, the colonel promised himself after two hours of waiting. But he waited twenty minutes more. He was getting set to leave when Sabas entered the office followed by a group of workers. He passed back and forth in front of the colonel without looking at him.

"Are you waiting for me, friend?"

"Yes, friend," the colonel said. "But if you're very busy, I can come back later."

Sabas didn't hear him from the other side of the door.

"I'll be right back," he said.

Noon was stifling. The office shone with the shimmering of the street. Dulled by the heat, the colonel involuntarily closed his eyes and at once began to dream of his wife. Sabas's wife came in on tiptoe.

"Don't wake up, friend," she said. "I'm going to draw the blinds because this office is an inferno."

The colonel followed her with a blank look. She spoke in the shadow when she closed the window.

"Do you dream often?"

"Sometimes," replied the colonel, ashamed of having fallen asleep. "Almost always I dream that I'm getting tangled up in spider webs."

"I have nightmares every night," the woman said. "Now I've got it in my head to find out who those unknown people are whom one meets in one's dreams."

She plugged in the fan. "Last week a woman appeared at the head of my bed," she said. "I managed to ask her who she was and she replied, 'I am the woman who died in this room twelve years ago.' "

"But the house was built barely two years ago," the colonel said.

"That's right," the woman said. "That means that even the dead make mistakes."

The hum of the fan solidified the shadow. The colonel felt impatient, tormented by sleepiness and by the rambling woman who went directly from dreams to the mystery of the reincarnation. He was waiting for a pause to say goodbye when Sabas entered the office with his foreman.

"I've warmed up your soup four times," the woman said.

"Warm it up ten times if you like," said Sabas. "But stop nagging me now."

He opened the safe and gave his foreman a roll of bills together with a list of instructions. The foreman opened the blinds to count the money. Sabas saw the colonel at the back of the office but didn't show any reaction. He kept talking with the foreman. The colonel straightened up at the point when the two men were getting ready to leave the office again. Sabas stopped before opening the door.

"What can I do for you, friend?"

The colonel saw that the foreman was looking at him.

"Nothing, friend," he said. "I just wanted to talk to you."

"Make it fast, whatever it is," said Sabas. "I don't have a minute to spare."

He hesitated with his hand resting on the doorknob. The colonel felt the five longest seconds of his life passing. He clenched his teeth.

"It's about the rooster," he murmured.

Then Sabas finished opening the door. "The question of the rooster," he repeated, smiling, and pushed the foreman toward the hall. "The sky is falling in and my friend is worrying about that rooster." And then, addressing the colonel:

"Very well, friend. I'll be right back."

The colonel stood motionless in the middle of the office until he could no longer hear the footsteps of the two men at the end of the hall. Then he went out to walk around the town which was paralyzed in its Sunday siesta. There was no one at the tailor's. The doctor's office was closed. No one was watching the goods set out at the Syrians' stalls. The river was a sheet of steel. A man at the waterfront was sleeping across four oil drums, his face protected from the sun by a hat. The colonel went home, certain that he was the only thing moving in town.

His wife was waiting for him with a complete lunch.

"I bought it on credit; promised to pay first thing tomorrow," she explained.

During lunch, the colonel told her the events of the last three hours. She listened to him impatiently.

"The trouble is you lack character," she said finally. "You present yourself as if you were begging alms when you ought to go there with you head high and take our friend aside and say, 'Friend, I've decided to sell you the rooster.' "

"Life is a breeze the way you tell it," the colonel said.

She assumed an energetic attitude. That morning she had put the house in order and was dressed very strangely, in her husband's old shoes, and oilcloth apron, and a rag tied around her head with two knots at the ears. "You haven't the slightest sense for business," she said. "When you go to sell something, you have to put on the same face as when you go to buy."

The colonel found something amusing in her figure.

"Stay just the way you are," he interrupted her, smiling.

"You're identical to the little Quaker Oats man."

She took the rag off her head.

"I'm speaking seriously," she said. "I'm going to take the rooster to our friend right now, and I'll bet whatever you want that I come back inside of half an hour with the nine hundred pesos."

"You've got zeros on the brain," the colonel said. "You're already betting with the money from the rooster."

It took a lot of trouble for him to dissuade her. She had spent the morning mentally organizing the budget for the next three years without their Friday agony. She had made a list of the essentials they needed, without forgetting a pair of new shoes for the colonel. She set aside a place in the bedroom for the mirror. The momentary frustration of her plans left her with a confused sensation of shame and resentment.

She took a short siesta. When she got up, the colonel was sitting in the patio.

"Now what are you doing?" she asked.

"I'm thinking," the colonel said.

"Then the problem is solved. We will be able to count on that money fifty years from now."

But in reality the colonel had decided to sell the rooster that very afternoon. He thought of Sabas, alone in his office, preparing himself for his daily injection in front of the electric fan. He had his answer ready.

"Take the rooster," his wife advised him as he went out. "Seeing him in the flesh will work a miracle."

The colonel objected. She followed him to the front door with desperate anxiety.

"It doesn't matter if the whole army is in the office," she said. "You grab him by the arm and don't let him move until he gives you the nine hundred pesos."

"They'll think we're planning a hold-up."

She paid no attention.

"Remember that you are the owner of the rooster," she insisted. "Remember that you are the one who's going to do him the favor."

"All right."

Sabas was in the bedroom with the doctor. "Now's your chance, friend," his wife said to the colonel. "The doctor is getting him ready to travel to the ranch, and he's not coming back until Thursday." The colonel struggled with two opposing forces: in spite of his determination to sell the rooster, he wished he had arrived an hour later and missed Sabas.

"I can wait," he said.

But the woman insisted. She led him to the bedroom where her husband was seated on the throne-like bed, in his underwear, his colorless eyes fixed on the doctor. The colonel waited until the doctor had heated the glass tube with the patient's urine, sniffed the odor, and made an approving gesture to Sabas.

"We'll have to shoot him," the doctor said, turning to the colonel. "Diabetes is too slow for finishing off the wealthy."

"You've already done your best with your damned insulin injections," said Sabas, and he gave a jump on his flaccid buttocks. "But I'm a hard nut to crack." And then, to the colonel:

"Come in, friend. When I went out to look for you this afternoon, I couldn't even see your hat."

"I don't wear one, so I won't have to take it off for anyone."

Sabas began to get dressed. The doctor put a glass tube with a blood sample in his jacket pocket. Then he straightened out the things in his bag. The colonel thought he was getting ready to leave.

"If I were in your shoes, I'd send my friend a bill for a hundred thousand pesos, Doctor," the colonel said. "That way he wouldn't be so worried."

"I've already suggested that to him, but for a million," the doctor said. "Poverty is the best cure for diabetes."

"Thanks for the prescription," said Sabas, trying to stuff his voluminous belly into his riding breeches. "But I won't accept it, to save you from the catastrophe of becoming rich." The doctor saw his own teeth reflected in the little chromed lock of his bag. He looked at the clock without showing impatience. Sabas, putting on his boots, suddenly turned to the colonel:

"Well, friend, what's happening with the rooster?"

The colonel realized that the doctor was also waiting for his answer. He clenched his teeth.

"Nothing, friend," he murmured. "I've come to sell him to you."

Sabas finished putting on his boots.

"Fine, my friend," he said without emotion. "It's the most sensible thing that could have occurred to you."

"I'm too old now for these complications," the colonel said to justify himself before the doctor's impenetrable expression. "If I were twenty years younger it would be different."

"You'll always be twenty years younger," the doctor replied.

The colonel regained his breath. He waited for Sabas to say something more, but he didn't. Sabas put on a leather zippered jacket and got ready to leave the bedroom.

"If you like, we'll talk about it next week, friend," the colonel said.

"That's what I was going to say," said Sabas. "I have a customer who might give you four hundred pesos. But we have to wait till Thursday."

"How much?" the doctor asked.

"Four hundred pesos."

"I had heard someone say that he was worth a lot more," the doctor said.

"You were talking in terms of nine hundred pesos," the

colonel said, backed by the doctor's perplexity. "He's the best rooster in the whole province."

Sabas answered the doctor.

"At some other time, anyone would have paid a thousand," he explained. "But now no one dares pit a good rooster. There's always the danger he'll come out of the pit shot to death." He turned to the colonel, feigning disappointment:

"That's what I wanted to tell you, friend."

The colonel nodded.

"Fine," he said.

He followed him down the hall. The doctor stayed in the living room, detained by Sabas's wife, who asked him for a remedy "for those things which come over one suddenly and which one doesn't know what they are." The colonel waited for him in the office. Sabas opened the safe, stuffed money into all his pockets, and held out four bills to the colonel.

"There's sixty pesos, friend," he said. "When the rooster is sold we'll settle up."

The colonel walked with the doctor past the stalls at the waterfront, which were beginning to revive in the cool of the afternoon. A barge loaded with sugar cane was moving down the thread of current. The colonel found the doctor strangely impervious.

"And you, how are you, Doctor?"

The doctor shrugged.

"As usual," he said. "I think I need a doctor."

"It's the winter," the colonel said. "It eats away my insides."

The doctor examined him with a look absolutely devoid of any professional interest. In succession he greeted the Syrians seated at the doors of their shops. At the door of the doctor's office, the colonel expressed his opinion of the sale of the rooster.

"I couldn't do anything else," he explained. "That animal feeds on human flesh."

"The only animal who feeds on human flesh is Sabas," the doctor said. "I'm sure he'd resell the rooster for the nine hundred pesos."

"You think so?"

"I'm sure of it," the doctor said. "It's as sweet a deal as his famous patriotic pact with the Mayor."

The colonel refused to believe it. "My friend made that pact to save his skin," he said. "That's how he could stay in town."

"And that's how he could buy the property of his fellow-partisans whom the Mayor kicked out at half their price," the doctor replied. He knocked on the door, since he didn't find his keys in his pockets. Then he faced the colonel's disbelief. "Don't be so naïve," he said. "Sabas is much more interested in money than in his own skin."

The colonel's wife went shopping that night. He accompanied her to the Syrians' stalls, pondering the doctor's revelations.

"Find the boys immediately and tell them that the rooster is sold," she told him. "We mustn't leave them with any hopes."

"The rooster won't be sold until my friend Sabas comes back," the colonel answered.

He found Alvaro playing roulette in the pool hall. The place was sweltering on Sunday night. The heat seemed more intense because of the vibrations of the radio turned up full blast. The colonel amused himself with the brightly colored numbers painted on a large black oilcloth cover and lit by an oil lantern placed on a box in the center of the table. Alvaro insisted on losing on twenty-three. Following the game over his shoulder, the colonel observed that the eleven turned up four times in nine spins.

"Bet on eleven," he whispered into Alvaro's ear. "It's the one coming up most."

Alvaro examined the table. He didn't bet on the next spin. He took some money out of his pants pocket, and with it a sheet of paper. He gave the paper to the colonel under the table.

"It's from Agustín," he said.

The colonel put the clandestine note in his pocket. Alvaro bet heavily on the eleven.

"Start with just a little," the colonel said.

"It may be a good hunch," Alvaro replied. A group of neighboring players took their bets off the other numbers and bet on eleven after the enormous colored wheel had already begun to turn. The colonel felt oppressed. For the first time he felt the fascination, agitation, and bitterness of gambling.

The five won.

"I'm sorry," the colonel said, ashamed, and, with an irresistible feeling of guilt, followed the little wooden rake which pulled in Alvaro's money. "That's what I get for butting into what doesn't concern me."

Alvaro smiled without looking at him.

"Don't worry, Colonel. Trust to love."

The trumpets playing a mambo were suddenly interrupted. The gamblers scattered with their hands in the air. The colonel felt the dry snap, articulate and cold, of a rifle being cocked behind his back. He realized that he had been caught fatally in a police raid with the clandestine paper in his pocket. He turned halfway around without raising his hands. And then he saw, close up, for the first time in his life, the man who had shot his son. The man was directly in front of him, with his rifle barrel aimed at the colonel's belly. He was small, Indian-looking, with weather-beaten skin, and his breath smelled like a child's. The colonel gritted his teeth and gently pushed the rifle barrel away with the tips of his fingers.

"Excuse me," he said.

He confronted two round little bat eyes. In an instant, he

felt himself being swallowed up by those eyes, crushed, digested, and expelled immediately.

"You may go, Colonel."

He didn't need to open the window to tell it was December. He knew it in his bones when he was cutting up the fruit for the rooster's breakfast in the kitchen. Then he opened the door and the sight of the patio confirmed his feeling. It was a marvelous patio, with the grass and the trees, and the cubicle with the privy floating in the clear air, one millimeter above the ground.

His wife stayed in bed until nine. When she appeared in the kitchen, the colonel had already straightened up the house and was talking to the children in a circle around the rooster. She had to make a detour to get to the stove.

"Get out of the way!" she shouted. She glowered in the animal's direction. "I don't know when I'll ever get rid of that evil-omened bird."

The colonel regarded his wife's mood over the rooster. Nothing about the rooster deserved resentment. He was ready for training. His neck and his feathered purple thighs, his sawtoothed crest: the animal had taken on a slender figure, a defenseless air.

"Lean out the window and forget the rooster," the colonel said when the children left. "On mornings like this, one feels like having a picture taken."

She leaned out the window but her face betrayed no emotion. "I would like to plant the roses," she said, returning to the stove. The colonel hung the mirror on the hook to shave.

"If you want to plant the roses, go ahead," he said.

He tried to make his movements match those in the mirror.

"The pigs eat them up," she said.

"All the better," the colonel said. "Pigs fattened on roses ought to taste very good."

He looked for his wife in the mirror and noticed that she still had the same expression. By the light of the fire her face seemed to be formed of the same material as the stove. Without noticing, his eyes fixed on her, the colonel continued shaving himself by touch as he had done for many years. The woman thought, in a long silence.

"But I don't want to plant them," she said.

"Fine," said the colonel. "Then don't plant them."

He felt well. December had shriveled the flora in his gut. He suffered a disappointment that morning trying to put on his new shoes. But after trying several times he realized that it was a wasted effort, and put on his patent-leather ones. His wife noticed the change.

"If you don't put on the new ones you'll never break them in," she said.

"They're shoes for a cripple," the colonel protested. "They ought to sell shoes that have already been worn for a month."

He went into the street stimulated by the presentiment that the letter would arrive that afternoon. Since it still was not time for the launches, he waited for Sabas in his office. But they informed him that he wouldn't be back until Monday. He didn't lose his patience despite not having foreseen this setback. "Sooner or later he has to come back," he told himself, and he headed for the harbor; it was a marvelous moment, a moment of still-unblemished clarity.

"The whole year ought to be December," he murmured, seated in the store of Moses the Syrian. "One feels as if he were made of glass."

Moses the Syrian had to make an effort to translate the idea into his almost forgotten Arabic. He was a placid Oriental, encased up to his ears in smooth, stretched skin, and he had the clumsy movements of a drowned man. In fact, he seemed as if he had just been rescued from the water.

"That's the way it was before," he said. "If it were the same now, I would be eight hundred and ninety-seven years old. And you?"

"Seventy-five," said the colonel, his eyes pursuing the postmaster. Only then did he discover the circus. He recognized the patched tent on the roof of the mail boat amid a pile of colored objects. For a second he lost the postmaster while he looked for the wild animals among the crates piled up on the other launches. He didn't find them.

"It's a circus," he said. "It's the first one that's come in ten years."

Moses the Syrian verified his report. He spoke to his wife in a pidgin of Arabic and Spanish. She replied from the back of the store. He made a comment to himself, and then translated his worry for the colonel.

"Hide your cat, Colonel. The boys will steal it to sell it to the circus."

The colonel was getting ready to follow the postmaster.

"It's not a wild-animal show," he said.

"It doesn't matter," the Syrian replied. "The tightrope walkers eat cats so they won't break their bones."

He followed the postmaster through the stalls at the waterfront to the plaza. There the loud clamor from the cockfight took him by surprise. A passer-by said something to him about his rooster. Only then did he remember that this was the day set for the trials.

He passed the post office. A moment later he had sunk into the turbulent atmosphere of the pit. He saw his rooster in the middle of the pit, alone, defenseless, his spurs wrapped in rags, with something like fear visible in the trembling of his feet. His adversary was a sad ashen rooster.

The colonel felt no emotion. There was a succession of identical attacks. A momentary engagement of feathers and feet and necks in the middle of an enthusiastic ovation. Knocked against the planks of the barrier, the adversary did a somersault and returned to the attack. His rooster didn't attack. He rebuffed every attack, and landed again in exactly the same spot. But now his feet weren't trembling.

Hernán jumped the barrier, picked him up with both hands, and showed him to the crowd in the stands. There was a frenetic explosion of applause and shouting. The colonel noticed the disproportion between the enthusiasm of the applause and the intensity of the fight. It seemed to him a farce to which—voluntarily and consciously—the roosters had also lent themselves.

Impelled by a slightly disdainful curiosity, he examined the circular pit. An excited crowd was hurtling down the stands toward the pit. The colonel observed the confusion of hot, anxious, terribly alive faces. They were new people. All the new people in town. He relived—with foreboding—an instant which had been erased on the edge of his memory. Then he leaped the barrier, made his way through the packed crowd in the pit, and confronted Hernán's calm eyes. They looked at each other without blinking.

"Good afternoon, Colonel."

The colonel took the rooster away from him. "Good afternoon," he muttered. And he said nothing more because the warm deep throbbing of the animal made him shudder. He thought that he had never had such an alive thing in his hands before.

"You weren't at home," Hernán said, confused.

A new ovation interrupted him. The colonel felt intimidated. He made his way again, without looking at anybody, stunned by the applause and the shouts, and went into the street with his rooster under his arm.

The whole town—the lower-class people—came out to watch him go by followed by the school children. A gigantic Negro standing on a table with a snake wrapped around his neck was selling medicine without a license at a corner of the plaza. A large group returning from the harbor had stopped to listen to his spiel. But when the colonel passed with the rooster, their attention shifted to him. The way home had never been so long.

He had no regrets. For a long time the town had lain in a sort of stupor, ravaged by ten years of history. That afternoon —another Friday without a letter—the people had awakened. The colonel remembered another era. He saw himself with his wife and his son watching under an umbrella a show which was not interrupted despite the rain. He remembered the party's leaders, scrupulously groomed, fanning themselves to the beat of the music in the patio of his house. He almost relived the painful resonance of the bass drum in his intestines.

He walked along the street parallel to the harbor and there, too, found the tumultuous Election Sunday crowd of long ago. They were watching the circus unloading. From inside a tent, a woman shouted something about the rooster. He continued home, self-absorbed, still hearing scattered voices, as if the remnants of the ovation in the pit were pursuing him.

At the door he addressed the children:

"Everyone go home," he said. "Anyone who comes in will leave with a hiding."

He barred the door and went straight into the kitchen. His wife came out of the bedroom choking.

"They took it by force," she said, sobbing. "I told them that the rooster would not leave this house while I was alive." The colonel tied the rooster to the leg of the stove. He changed the water in the can, pursued by his wife's frantic voice.

"They said they would take it over our dead bodies," she said. "They said the rooster didn't belong to us but to the whole town."

Only when he finished with the rooster did the colonel turn to the contorted face of his wife. He discovered, without surprise, that it produced neither remorse nor compassion in him.

"They did the right thing," he said quietly. And then, looking through his pockets, he added with a sort of bottomless sweetness:

"The rooster's not for sale."

She followed him to the bedroom. She felt him to be completely human, but untouchable, as if she were seeing him on a movie screen. The colonel took a roll of bills out of the closet, added what he had in his pockets to it, counted the total, and put it back in the closet.

"There are twenty-nine pesos to return to my friend Sabas," he said. "He'll get the rest when the pension arrives."

"And if it doesn't arrive?" the woman asked.

"It will."

"But if it doesn't?"

"Well, then, he won't get paid."

He found his new shoes under the bed. He went back to the closet for the box, cleaned the soles with a rag, and put the shoes in the box, just as his wife had brought them Sunday night. She didn't move.

"The shoes go back," the colonel said. "That's thirteen pesos more for my friend."

"They won't take them back," she said.

"They have to take them back," the colonel replied. "I've only put them on twice."

"The Turks don't understand such things," the woman said.

"They have to understand."

"And if they don't?"

"Well, then, they don't."

They went to bed without eating. The colonel waited for his wife to finish her rosary to turn out the lamp. But he couldn't sleep. He heard the bells for the movie classifications, and almost at once—three hours later—the curfew. The gravelly breathing of his wife became anguished with the chilly night air. The colonel still had his eyes open when she spoke to him in a calm, conciliatory voice:

"You're awake."

"Yes."

"Try to listen to reason," the woman said. "Talk to my friend Sabas tomorrow."

"He's not coming back until Monday."

"Better," said the woman. "That way you'll have three days to think about what you're going to say."

"There's nothing to think about," the colonel said.

A pleasant coolness had taken the place of the viscous air of October. The colonel recognized December again in the timetable of the plovers. When it struck two, he still hadn't been able to fall asleep. But he knew that his wife was also awake. He tried to change his position in the hammock.

"You can't sleep," the woman said.

"No."

She thought for a moment.

"We're in no condition to do that," she said. "Just think how much four hundred pesos in one lump sum is."

"It won't be long now till the pension comes," the colonel said.

"You've been saying the same thing for fifteen years."

"That's why," the colonel said. "It can't be much longer now."

She was silent. But when she spoke again, it didn't seem to the colonel as if any time had passed at all.

"I have the impression the money will never arrive," the woman said.

"It will."

"And if it doesn't?"

He couldn't find his voice to answer. At the first crowing of the rooster he was struck by reality, but he sank back again into a dense, safe, remorseless sleep. When he awoke, the sun was already high in the sky. His wife was sleeping. The colonel methodically repeated his morning activities, two hours behind schedule, and waited for his wife to eat breakfast.

She was uncommunicative when she awoke. They said good morning, and they sat down to eat in silence. The colonel sipped a cup of black coffee and had a piece of cheese and a sweet roll. He spent the whole morning in the tailor shop. At one o'clock he returned home and found his wife mending clothes among the begonias.

"It's lunchtime," he said.

"There is no lunch."

He shrugged. He tried to block up the holes in the patio wall to prevent the children from coming into the kitchen. When he came back into the hall, lunch was on the table.

During the course of lunch, the colonel realized that his wife was making an effort not to cry. This certainty alarmed him. He knew his wife's character, naturally hard, and hardened even more by forty years of bitterness. The death of her son had not wrung a single tear out of her.

He fixed a reproving look directly on her eyes. She bit her lips, dried her eyelids on her sleeve, and continued eating lunch.

"You have no consideration," she said.

The colonel didn't speak.

"You're willful, stubborn, and inconsiderate," she repeated. She crossed her knife and fork on the plate, but immediately rectified their positions superstitiously. "An entire lifetime eating dirt just so that now it turns out that I deserve less consideration than a rooster."

"That's different," the colonel said.

"It's the same thing," the woman replied. "You ought to realize that I'm dying; this thing I have is not a sickness but a slow death."

The colonel didn't speak until he finished eating his lunch.

"If the doctor guarantees me that by selling the rooster you'll get rid of your asthma, I'll sell him immediately," he said. "But if not, not."

That afternoon he took the rooster to the pit. On his return he found his wife on the verge of an attack. She was walking up and down the hall, her hair down her back, her arms spread wide apart, trying to catch her breath above the whistling in her lungs. She was there until early evening. Then she went to bed without speaking to her husband.

She mouthed prayers until a little after curfew. Then the colonel got ready to put out the lamp. But she objected.

"I don't want to die in the dark," she said.

The colonel left the lamp on the floor. He began to feel exhausted. He wished he could forget everything, sleep forty-four days in one stretch, and wake up on January 20th at three in the afternoon, in the pit, and at the exact moment to let the rooster loose. But he felt himself threatened by the sleeplessness of his wife.

"It's the same story as always," she began a moment later. "We put up with hunger so others can eat. It's been the same story for forty years."

The colonel kept silent until his wife paused to ask him if he was awake. He answered that he was. The woman continued in a smooth, fluent, implacable tone.

"Everybody will win with the rooster except us. We're the only ones who don't have a cent to bet."

"The owner of the rooster is entitled to twenty per cent."

"You were also entitled to get a position when they made you break your back for them in the elections," the woman replied. "You were also entitled to the veteran's pension after risking your neck in the civil war. Now everyone has his future assured and you're dying of hunger, completely alone."

"I'm not alone," the colonel said.

He tried to explain, but sleep overtook him. She kept talking dully until she realized that her husband was sleeping. Then she got out of the mosquito net and walked up and down the living room in the darkness. There she continued talking. The colonel called her at dawn.

She appeared at the door, ghostlike, illuminated from below by the lamp which was almost out. She put it out before getting into the mosquito netting. But she kept talking.

"We're going to do one thing," the colonel interrupted her.

"The only thing we can do is sell the rooster," said the woman.

"We can also sell the clock."

"They won't buy it."

"Tomorrow I'll try to see if Alvaro will give me the forty pesos."

"He won't give them to you."

"Then we'll sell the picture."

When the woman spoke again, she was outside the mosquito net again. The colonel smelled her breath impregnated with medicinal herbs.

"They won't buy it," she said.

"We'll see," the colonel said gently, without a trace of change in his voice. "Now, go to sleep. If we can't sell anything tomorrow, we'll think of something else."

He tried to keep his eyes open but sleep broke his resolve. He fell to the bottom of a substance without time and without space, where the words of his wife had a different significance. But a moment later he felt himself being shaken by the shoulder.

"Answer me."

The colonel didn't know if he had heard those words before or after he had slept. Dawn was breaking. The window stood out in Sunday's green clarity. He thought he had a fever. His eyes burned and he had to make a great effort to clear his head.

"What will we do if we can't sell anything?" the woman repeated.

"By then it will be January 20th," the colonel said, completely awake. "They'll pay the twenty per cent that very afternoon."

"If the rooster wins," the woman said. "But if he loses. It hasn't occurred to you that the rooster might lose."

"He's one rooster that can't lose."

"But suppose he loses."

"There are still forty-four days left to begin to think about that," the colonel said.

The woman lost her patience.

"And meanwhile what do we eat?" she asked, and seized the colonel by the collar of his flannel night shirt. She shook him hard.

It had taken the colonel seventy-five years—the seventy-five years of his life, minute by minute—to reach this moment. He felt pure, explicit, invincible at the moment when he replied:

"Shit."

Big Mama's
Funeral

TUESDAY SIESTA

THE TRAIN emerged from the quivering tunnel of sandy rocks, began to cross the symmetrical, interminable banana plantations, and the air became humid and they couldn't feel the sea breeze any more. A stifling blast of smoke came in the car window. On the narrow road parallel to the railway there were oxcarts loaded with green bunches of bananas. Beyond the road, in uncultivated spaces set at odd intervals there were offices with electric fans, red-brick buildings, and residences with chairs and little white tables on the terraces among dusty palm trees and rosebushes. It was eleven in the morning, and the heat had not yet begun.

"You'd better close the window," the woman said. "Your hair will get full of soot."

The girl tried to, but the shade wouldn't move because of the rust.

They were the only passengers in the lone third-class car. Since the smoke of the locomotive kept coming through the window, the girl left her seat and put down the only things they had with them: a plastic sack with some things to eat and a bouquet of flowers wrapped in newspaper. She sat on the opposite seat, away from the window, facing her mother. They were both in severe and poor mourning clothes.

The girl was twelve years old, and it was the first time she'd ever been on a train. The woman seemed too old to be her mother, because of the blue veins on her eyelids and her small, soft, and shapeless body, in a dress cut like a cassock. She was riding with her spinal column braced firmly against the back of the seat, and held a peeling patent-leather handbag in her lap

with both hands. She bore the conscientious serenity of someone accustomed to poverty.

By twelve the heat had begun. The train stopped for ten
minutes to take on water at a station where there was no town.
Outside, in the mysterious silence of the plantations, the
shadows seemed clean. But the still air inside the car smelled
like untanned leather. The train did not pick up speed. It
stopped at two identical towns with wooden houses painted
bright colors. The woman's head nodded and she sank into
sleep. The girl took off her shoes. Then she went to the wash-
room to put the bouquet of flowers in some water.

When she came back to her seat, her mother was waiting to
eat. She gave her a piece of cheese, half a corn-meal pancake,
and a cookie, and took an equal portion out of the plastic sack
for herself. While they ate, the train crossed an iron bridge
very slowly and passed a town just like the ones before, except
that in this one there was a crowd in the plaza. A band was
playing a lively tune under the oppressive sun. At the other
side of town the plantations ended in a plain which was cracked
from the drought.

The woman stopped eating.

"Put on your shoes," she said.

The girl looked outside. She saw nothing but the deserted
plain, where the train began to pick up speed again, but she
put the last piece of cookie into the sack and quickly put on
her shoes. The woman gave her a comb.

"Comb your hair," she said.

The train whistle began to blow while the girl was combing
her hair. The woman dried the sweat from her neck and wiped
the oil from her face with her fingers. When the girl stopped
combing, the train was passing the outlying houses of a town
larger but sadder than the earlier ones.

"If you feel like doing anything, do it now," said the

woman. "Later, don't take a drink anywhere even if you're dying of thirst. Above all, no crying."

The girl nodded her head. A dry, burning wind came in the window, together with the locomotive's whistle and the clatter of the old cars. The woman folded the plastic bag with the rest of the food and put it in the handbag. For a moment a complete picture of the town, on that bright August Tuesday, shone in the window. The girl wrapped the flowers in the soaking-wet newspapers, moved a little farther away from the window, and stared at her mother. She received a pleasant expression in return. The train began to whistle and slowed down. A moment later it stopped.

There was no one at the station. On the other side of the street, on the sidewalk shaded by the almond trees, only the pool hall was open. The town was floating in the heat. The woman and the girl got off the train and crossed the abandoned station—the tiles split apart by the grass growing up between—and over to the shady side of the street.

It was almost two. At that hour, weighted down by drowsiness, the town was taking a siesta. The stores, the town offices, the public school were closed at eleven, and didn't reopen until a little before four, when the train went back. Only the hotel across from the station, with its bar and pool hall, and the telegraph office at one side of the plaza stayed open. The houses, most of them built on the banana company's model, had their doors locked from inside and their blinds drawn. In some of them it was so hot that the residents ate lunch in the patio. Others leaned a chair against the wall, in the shade of the almond trees, and took their siesta right out in the street.

Keeping to the protective shade of the almond trees, the woman and the girl entered the town without disturbing the siesta. They went directly to the parish house. The woman scratched the metal grating on the door with her fingernail, waited a moment, and scratched again. An electric fan was humming inside. They did not hear the steps. They hardly heard the slight creaking of a door, and immediately a cautious voice, right next to the metal grating: "Who is it?" The woman tried to see through the grating.

"I need the priest," she said.

"He's sleeping now."

"It's an emergency," the woman insisted.

Her voice showed a calm determination.

The door was opened a little way, noiselessly, and a plump, older woman appeared, with very pale skin and hair the color of iron. Her eyes seemed too small behind her thick eyeglasses.

"Come in," she said, and opened the door all the way.

They entered a room permeated with an old smell of flowers. The woman of the house led them to a wooden bench and signaled them to sit down. The girl did so, but her mother remained standing, absent-mindedly, with both hands clutching the handbag. No noise could be heard above the electric fan.

The woman of the house reappeared at the door at the far end of the room. "He says you should come back after three," she said in a very low voice. "He just lay down five minutes ago."

"The train leaves at three-thirty," said the woman.

It was a brief and self-assured reply, but her voice remained pleasant, full of undertones. The woman of the house smiled for the first time.

"All right," she said.

When the far door closed again, the woman sat down next to her daughter. The narrow waiting room was poor, neat, and clean. On the other side of the wooden railing which divided the room, there was a worktable, a plain one with an oilcloth cover, and on top of the table a primitive typewriter next to a vase of flowers. The parish records were beyond. You could see that it was an office kept in order by a spinster.

The far door opened and this time the priest appeared, cleaning his glasses with a handkerchief. Only when he put them on was it evident that he was the brother of the woman who had opened the door.

"How can I help you?" he asked.

"The keys to the cemetery," said the woman.

The girl was seated with the flowers in her lap and her feet crossed under the bench. The priest looked at her, then looked at the woman, and then through the wire mesh of the window at the bright, cloudless sky.

"In this heat," he said. "You could have waited until the sun went down."

The woman moved her head silently. The priest crossed to the other side of the railing, took out of the cabinet a notebook covered in oilcloth, a wooden penholder, and an inkwell, and sat down at the table. There was more than enough hair on his hands to account for what was missing on his head.

"Which grave are you going to visit?" he asked.

"Carlos Centeno's," said the woman.

"Who?"

"Carlos Centeno," the woman repeated.

The priest still did not understand.

"He's the thief who was killed here last week," said the woman in the same tone of voice. "I am his mother."

The priest scrutinized her. She stared at him with quiet self-control, and the Father blushed. He lowered his head and began to write. As he filled the page, he asked the woman to identify herself, and she replied unhesitatingly, with precise details, as if she were reading them. The Father began to sweat. The girl unhooked the buckle of her left shoe, slipped her heel out of it, and rested it on the bench rail. She did the same with the right one.

It had all started the Monday of the previous week, at three in the morning, a few blocks from there. Rebecca, a lonely widow who lived in a house full of odds and ends, heard above the sound of the drizzling rain someone trying to force the front door from outside. She got up, rummaged around in her closet for an ancient revolver that no one had fired since the days of Colonel Aureliano Buendía, and went into the living room without turning on the lights. Orienting herself not so much by the noise at the lock as by a terror developed in her by twenty-eight years of loneliness, she fixed in her imagination not only the spot where the door was but also the exact height of the lock. She clutched the weapon with both hands, closed her eyes, and squeezed the trigger. It was the first time in her life that she had fired a gun. Immediately after the explosion, she could hear nothing except the murmur of the drizzle on the galvanized roof. Then she heard a little metallic bump on the cement porch, and a very low voice, pleasant but terribly exhausted: "Ah, Mother." The man they found dead in front of the house in the morning, his nose blown to bits, wore a flannel shirt with colored stripes, everyday pants with a rope for a belt, and was barefoot. No one in town knew him.

"So his name was Carlos Centeno," murmured the Father when he finished writing.

"Centeno Ayala," said the woman. "He was my only boy."

The priest went back to the cabinet. Two big rusty keys hung on the inside of the door; the girl imagined, as her mother had when she was a girl and as the priest himself must have imagined at some time, that they were Saint Peter's keys. He took them down, put them on the open notebook on the railing, and pointed with his forefinger to a place on the page he had just written, looking at the woman.

"Sign here."

The woman scribbled her name, holding the handbag under her arm. The girl picked up the flowers, came to the railing shuffling her feet, and watched her mother attentively.

The priest sighed.

"Didn't you ever try to get him on the right track?"

The woman answered when she finished signing.

"He was a very good man."

The priest looked first at the woman and then at the girl, and realized with a kind of pious amazement that they were not about to cry. The woman continued in the same tone:

"I told him never to steal anything that anyone needed to eat, and he minded me. On the other hand, before, when he used to box, he used to spend three days in bed, exhausted from being punched."

"All his teeth had to be pulled out," interrupted the girl.

"That's right," the woman agreed. "Every mouthful I ate those days tasted of the beatings my son got on Saturday nights."

"God's will is inscrutable," said the Father.

But he said it without much conviction, partly because experience had made him a little skeptical and partly because of the heat. He suggested that they cover their heads to guard against sunstroke. Yawning, and now almost completely asleep, he gave them instructions about how to find Carlos Centeno's grave. When they came back, they didn't have to knock. They should put the key under the door; and in the same place, if they could, they should put an offering for the Church. The woman listened to his directions with great attention, but thanked him without smiling.

The Father had noticed that there was someone looking inside, his nose pressed against the metal grating, even before he opened the door to the street. Outside was a group of children. When the door was opened wide, the children scattered. Ordinarily, at that hour there was no one in the street. Now there were not only children. There were groups of people under the almond trees. The Father scanned the street swimming in the heat and then he understood. Softly, he closed the door again.

"Wait a moment," he said without looking at the woman.

His sister appeared at the far door with a black jacket over her nightshirt and her hair down over her shoulders. She looked silently at the Father.

"What was it?" he asked.

"The people have noticed," murmured his sister.

"You'd better go out by the door to the patio," said the Father.

"It's the same there," said his sister. "Everybody is at the windows."

The woman seemed not to have understood until then. She tried to look into the street through the metal grating. Then she took the bouquet of flowers from the girl and began to move toward the door. The girl followed her.

"Wait until the sun goes down," said the Father.

"You'll melt," said his sister, motionless at the back of the room. "Wait and I'll lend you a parasol."

"Thank you," replied the woman. "We're all right this way."

She took the girl by the hand and went into the street.

ONE OF THESE DAYS

MONDAY DAWNED warm and rainless. Aurelio Escovar, a dentist without a degree, and a very early riser, opened his office at six. He took some false teeth, still mounted in their plaster mold, out of the glass case and put on the table a fistful of instruments which he arranged in size order, as if they were on display. He wore a collarless striped shirt, closed at the neck with a golden stud, and pants held up by suspenders. He was erect and skinny, with a look that rarely corresponded to the situation, the way deaf people have of looking.

When he had things arranged on the table, he pulled the drill toward the dental chair and sat down to polish the false teeth. He seemed not to be thinking about what he was doing, but worked steadily, pumping the drill with his feet, even when he didn't need it.

After eight he stopped for a while to look at the sky through the window, and he saw two pensive buzzards who were drying themselves in the sun on the ridgepole of the house next door. He went on working with the idea that before lunch it would rain again. The shrill voice of his eleven-year-old son interrupted his concentration.

"Papá."

"What?"

"The Mayor wants to know if you'll pull his tooth."

"Tell him I'm not here."

He was polishing a gold tooth. He held it at arm's length, and examined it with his eyes half closed. His son shouted again from the little waiting room.

"He says you are, too, because he can hear you."

73

The dentist kept examining the tooth. Only when he had put it on the table with the finished work did he say:

"So much the better."

He operated the drill again. He took several pieces of a bridge out of a cardboard box where he kept the things he still had to do and began to polish the gold.

"Papá."

"What?"

He still hadn't changed his expression.

"He says if you don't take out his tooth, he'll shoot you."

Without hurrying, with an extremely tranquil movement, he stopped pedaling the drill, pushed it away from the chair, and pulled the lower drawer of the table all the way out. There was a revolver. "O.K.," he said. "Tell him to come and shoot me."

He rolled the chair over opposite the door, his hand resting on the edge of the drawer. The Mayor appeared at the door. He had shaved the left side of his face, but the other side, swollen and in pain, had a five-day-old beard. The dentist saw many nights of desperation in his dull eyes. He closed the drawer with his fingertips and said softly:

"Sit down."

"Good morning," said the Mayor.

"Morning," said the dentist.

While the instruments were boiling, the Mayor leaned his skull on the headrest of the chair and felt better. His breath was icy. It was a poor office: an old wooden chair, the pedal drill, a glass case with ceramic bottles. Opposite the chair was a window with a shoulder-high cloth curtain. When he felt the dentist approach, the Mayor braced his heels and opened his mouth.

Aurelio Escovar turned his head toward the light. After inspecting the infected tooth, he closed the Mayor's jaw with a cautious pressure of his fingers.

"It has to be without anesthesia," he said.

"Why?"

"Because you have an abscess."

The Mayor looked him in the eye. "All right," he said, and tried to smile. The dentist did not return the smile. He brought the basin of sterilized instruments to the worktable and took them out of the water with a pair of cold tweezers, still without hurrying. Then he pushed the spittoon with the tip of his shoe, and went to wash his hands in the washbasin. He did all this without looking at the Mayor. But the Mayor didn't take his eyes off him.

It was a lower wisdom tooth. The dentist spread his feet and grasped the tooth with the hot forceps. The Mayor seized the arms of the chair, braced his feet with all his strength, and felt an icy void in his kidneys, but didn't make a sound. The dentist moved only his wrist. Without rancor, rather with a bitter tenderness, he said:

"Now you'll pay for our twenty dead men."

The Mayor felt the crunch of bones in his jaw, and his eyes filled with tears. But he didn't breathe until he felt the tooth come out. Then he saw it through his tears. It seemed so foreign to his pain that he failed to understand his torture of the five previous nights.

Bent over the spittoon, sweating, panting, he unbuttoned his tunic and reached for the handkerchief in his pants pocket. The dentist gave him a clean cloth.

"Dry your tears," he said.

The Mayor did. He was trembling. While the dentist washed his hands, he saw the crumbling ceiling and a dusty spider web with spider's eggs and dead insects. The dentist returned, drying his hands. "Go to bed," he said, "and gargle with salt water." The Mayor stood up, said goodbye with a casual military salute, and walked toward the door, stretching his legs, without buttoning up his tunic.

"Send the bill," he said.

"To you or the town?"

The Mayor didn't look at him. He closed the door and said through the screen:

"It's the same damn thing."

THERE ARE NO THIEVES
IN *THIS* TOWN

DAMASO CAME back to the room at the crack of dawn. Ana, his wife, six months pregnant, was waiting for him seated on the bed, dressed and with her shoes on. The oil lamp began to go out. Damaso realized that his wife had been waiting for him every minute through the whole night, and even now, at that moment when she could see him in front of her, was waiting still. He made a quieting gesture which she didn't reply to. She fixed her frightened eyes on the bundle of red cloth which he carried in his hand, pressed her lips together, and began to tremble. Damaso caught her by the chemise with a silent violence. He exhaled a bitter odor.

Ana let him lift her almost up in the air. Then she threw all the weight of her body forward, crying against her husband's red-striped flannel shirt, and clutched him around the kidneys until she managed to calm down.

"I fell asleep sitting up," she said. "Suddenly the door opened and you were pushed into the room, drenched with blood."

Damaso held her at arm's length without saying anything. He set her down on the bed again. Then he put the bundle in her lap and went out to urinate in the patio. She untied the string and saw that there were three billiard balls, two white ones and a red one, dull and very worn from use.

When he returned to the room, Damaso found her in deep thought.

"And what good is this?" Ana asked.

He shrugged his shoulders.

"To play billiards."

He tied the bundle up again and put it, together with the

77

homemade skeleton key, the flashlight, and the knife, in the bottom of the trunk. Ana lay down facing the wall without taking off her clothes. Damaso took off only his pants. Stretched out in bed, smoking in the darkness, he tried to recognize some trace of his adventure in the scattered rustlings of the dawn, until he realized that his wife was awake.

"What are you thinking about?"

"Nothing," she said.

Her voice, ordinarily a low contralto, seemed thicker because of her rancor. Damaso took one last puff on the cigarette and stubbed out the butt on the earthen floor.

"There was nothing else." He sighed. "I was inside about an hour."

"They might have shot you," she said.

Damaso trembled. "Damn you," he said, rapping the wooden bedframe with his knuckles. He felt around on the floor for his cigarettes and matches.

"You have the feelings of a donkey," Ana said. "You should have remembered that I was here, unable to sleep, thinking that you were being brought home dead every time there was a noise in the street." She added with a sigh:

"And all that just to end up with three billiard balls."

"There was nothing but twenty-five cents in the drawer."

"Then you shouldn't have taken anything."

"The hard part was getting in," said Damaso. "I couldn't come back empty-handed."

"You could have taken anything else."

"There was nothing else," said Damaso.

"No place has as many things as the pool hall."

"So it would seem," said Damaso. "But then, when you are inside there, you start to look at the things and to search all over, and you realize that there's nothing that's worth anything."

She was silent for a long time. Damaso imagined her with her eyes open, trying to find some object of value in the darkness of memory.

"Perhaps," she said.

Damaso lit up again. The alcohol was leaving him, in concentric waves, and he assumed once more the weight, the volume, and the responsibility of his limbs. "There was a cat there," he said. "An enormous white cat." Ana turned around, pressed her swollen belly against her husband's, and put her leg between his knees. She smelled of onion.

"Were you very frightened?"

"Me?"

"You," said Ana. "They say men get frightened, too."

He felt her smile, and he smiled. "A little," he said. "I had to piss so bad I couldn't stand it." He let himself be kissed without kissing her back. Then, conscious of the risks, but without regretting it, as if evoking the memories of a trip, he told her the details of his adventure.

She spoke after a long silence.

"It was crazy."

"It's all a question of starting," said Damaso, closing his eyes. "Besides, it didn't turn out so bad for a first attempt."

The sun's heat was late in coming. When Damaso woke up, his wife had been up for a while. He put his head under the faucet in the patio and held it there a few minutes until he was fully awake. The room was part of a gallery of similar and separate rooms, with a common patio crossed by clotheslines. Against the back wall, separated from the patio by a tin partition, Ana had set up a portable stove for cooking and for heating her irons, and a little table for eating and ironing. When she saw her husband approach, she put the ironed clothes to one side and took the irons off the stove so she

80 Gabriel García Márquez

could heat the coffee. She was older than he, with very pale skin, and her movements had the gentle efficiency of people who are used to reality.

Through the fog of his headache, Damaso realized that his wife wanted to tell him something with her look. Until then, he hadn't paid any attention to the voices in the patio.

"They haven't been talking about anything else all morning," murmured Ana, giving him his coffee. "The men went over there a little while ago."

Damaso saw for himself that the men and children had disappeared from the patio. While he drank his coffee, he silently followed the conversation of the women who were hanging their clothes in the sun. Finally he lit a cigarette and left the kitchen.

"Teresa," he called.

A girl with her clothes wet, plastered to her body, replied to his call. "Be careful," murmured Ana. The girl came over.

"What's going on?" asked Damaso.

"Someone got into the pool hall and walked off with everything," the girl said.

She seemed to know all the details. She explained how they had taken the place apart, piece by piece, and had even carried off the billiard table. She spoke with such conviction that Damaso could not believe it wasn't true.

"Shit," he said, coming back to the kitchen.

Ana began to sing between clenched teeth. Damaso leaned a chair against the patio wall, trying to repress his anxiety. Three months before, when he had turned twenty, the line of his mustache, cared for not only with a secret sense of sacrifice but also with a certain tenderness, had added a touch of maturity to his pockmarked face. Since then he had felt like an adult. But this morning, with the memories of the night before floating in the swamp of his headache, he could not find where to begin to live.

When she finished ironing, Ana put the clean clothes into two equal piles and got ready to go out.

"Don't be gone long," said Damaso.

"The usual."

He followed her into the room. "I left your plaid shirt there," Ana said. "You'd better not wear the striped one again." She confronted her husband's clear cat's eyes.

"We don't know if anyone saw you."

Damaso dried the sweat from his hands on his pants.

"No one saw me."

"We don't know," Ana repeated. She was carrying a bundle of clothes in each arm. "Besides, it's better for you not to go out. Wait until I take a little stroll around there as if I weren't interested."

In town people were talking of nothing else. Ana had to listen to the details of the same event several times, in different and contradictory versions. When she finished delivering the clothes, instead of going to the market as she did every Saturday, she went straight to the plaza.

She found fewer people in front of the pool hall than she had imagined. Some men were talking in the shade of the almond trees. The Syrians had put away their colored cloth for lunch, and the stores seemed to be dozing under the canvas awnings. A man was sleeping sprawled in a rocking chair, with his lips and legs wide apart, in the hotel lobby. Everything was paralyzed in the noonday heat.

Ana continued along by the pool hall, and when she passed the empty lot opposite the docks, she found the crowd. Then she remembered something Damaso had told her, which everybody knew but which only the customers of the place could have remembered: the rear door of the pool hall faced the empty lot. A moment later, folding her arms over her belly, she mingled with the crowd, her eyes fixed on the door that had been forced. The lock was intact but one of the staples had been pulled out like a tooth. For a moment Ana regarded the damage caused by that solitary and modest effort and thought about her husband with a feeling of pity.

"Who was it?" she asked.

She didn't dare look around.

They answered her, "No one knows. They say it was a stranger."

"It had to be," said a woman behind her. "There are no thieves in this town. Everybody knows everybody else."

Ana turned her head. "That's right," she said, smiling. She was covered with sweat. There was a very old man next to her with wrinkles on the back of his neck.

"Did they take everything?" she asked.

"Two hundred pesos, and the billiard balls," the old man said. He looked at her with unusual interest. "Pretty soon we'll have to sleep with our eyes open."

Ana looked away. "That's right," she said again. She put a cloth over her head, moving off, without being able to avoid the impression that the old man was still looking at her.

For a quarter of an hour the crowd jammed into the empty lot behaved respectfully, as if there were a dead person behind the broken door. Then it became agitated, turned around, and spilled out into the plaza.

The owner of the pool hall was at the front door, with the Mayor and two policemen. Short and rotund, his pants held up only by the pressure of his stomach, and with eyeglasses like those that children make, the owner seemed endowed with an overwhelming dignity.

The crowd surrounded him. Leaning against the wall, Ana listened to his report until the crowd began to disperse. Then, sweltering in the heat, she returned to her room in the middle of a noisy demonstration by the neighbors.

Stretched out in bed, Damaso had asked himself many times how Ana had managed to wait for him the night before without smoking. When he saw her enter, smiling, taking from her head the cloth covered with sweat, he squashed the almost un-smoked cigarette on the earthen floor, in the middle of a line of butts, and waited with increased anxiety.

"Well?"

Ana kneeled next to the bed.

"Well, besides being a thief, you're a liar," she said.

"Why?"

"Because you told me there was nothing in the drawer."

Damaso frowned.

"There was nothing."

"There were two hundred pesos," said Ana.

"That's a lie," he replied, raising his voice. Sitting up in bed, he regained his confidential tone. "There was only twenty-five cents."

He convinced her. "He's an old crook," said Damaso, clenching his fists. "He's looking for me to smash his face in."

Ana laughed out loud.

"Don't be stupid."

He ended up laughing, too. While he was shaving, his wife told him what she had been able to find out. The police were looking for a stranger. "They say he arrived Thursday and that they saw him last night walking around the docks," she said. "They say they can't find him anywhere." Damaso thought about the stranger whom he'd never seen; for an instant he was really convinced, and suspected him.

"He may have gone away," said Ana.

As always, Damaso needed three hours to get dressed. First came the precise trimming of his mustache. Then his bath under the faucet in the patio. With an interest which nothing had diminished since the night she saw him for the first time, Ana followed step by step the laborious process of his combing his hair. When she saw him looking at himself in the mirror before he went out, with his red plaid shirt on, Ana felt old and sloppy. Damaso jabbed at her with the agility of a professional boxer. She caught him by the wrists.

"Do you have any money?"

"I'm rich," answered Damaso in good humor. "I've got the two hundred pesos."

Ana turned toward the wall, took a roll of bills out of her bosom, and gave a peso to her husband, saying:

"Take it, Valentino."

That night Damaso was in the plaza with a group of his friends. The people who came in from the country with things to sell at Sunday's market were putting up their awnings amid the stands which sold French fries and lottery tickets, and from early evening on you could hear them snoring. Damaso's friends didn't seem any more interested in the theft at the pool hall than in the radio broadcast of the baseball championship, which they couldn't hear that night because the pool hall was closed. Talking about baseball, they went to the movie without previously deciding to or finding out about what was playing.

They were showing a movie with Cantinflas. In the first row of the balcony Damaso laughed shamelessly. He felt as if he were convalescing from his emotions. It was a pleasant June night, and in the empty stretches when you could see only the haze of the projector, the silence of the stars weighed in upon the roofless theater.

All at once the images on the screen went dim and there was a clatter at the back of the orchestra. In the sudden brightness, Damaso felt discovered, accused, and tried to run. But immediately he saw the audience in the orchestra paralyzed, and a policeman, his belt rolled around his fist, ferociously beating a man with the heavy copper buckle. He was a gigantic Negro. The women began to scream, and the policeman who was beating the Negro shouted over the women, "Thief! Thief!" The Negro rolled between the row of chairs, chased by two policemen who struck at his kidneys until they managed to grab him from behind. Then the one who had thrashed him tied his elbows behind his back with a strap, and the three of them pushed him toward the door. The thing happened so quickly that Damaso understood what had happened only when the Negro passed next to him, his shirt torn and his face smeared with a mixture of dust, sweat, and blood, sobbing, "Murderers, murderers." Then they turned on the projector and the film continued.

Damaso didn't laugh again. He saw snatches of a disconnected story, chain-smoking, until the lights went on and the spectators looked at each other as if they were frightened by reality. "That was good!" someone beside him exclaimed. Damaso didn't look at him.

"Cantinflas is very good," he said.

The current of people carried him to the door. The food hawkers, loaded with baskets, were going home. It was after eleven, but there were a lot of people in the street waiting for them to come out of the movie to find out about the Negro's capture.

That night Damaso entered the room so cautiously that when Ana, who was half asleep, noticed him, he was smoking his second cigarette, stretched out in bed.

"The food is on the stove," she said.

"I'm not hungry," said Damaso.

Ana sighed. "I dreamed that Nora was making puppets out of butter," she said, still without waking up. Suddenly she realized that she had fallen asleep without intending to, and turned toward Damaso, dazed, rubbing her eyes.

"They caught the stranger," she said.

Damaso waited before he spoke.

"Who said?"

"They caught him at the movie," said Ana. "Everyone is over there."

She related a distorted version of the arrest. Damaso didn't correct her.

"Poor man." Ana sighed.

"Why poor?" protested Damaso heatedly. "So you would rather have me be the one in the trap."

She knew him too well to reply. She sensed him smoking, breathing like an asthmatic, until the first light of dawn. Then she felt him out of bed, turning the room upside down in some obscure pursuit which seemed to depend on touch rather than sight. Then she felt him scraping the floor under the bed for more than fifteen minutes, and then she felt him undress in the darkness, trying not to make noise, without realizing that she hadn't stopped helping him for a second by making him think she was asleep. Something stirred in her most primitive instincts. Ana knew then that Damaso had been at the movie, and understood why he had just buried the billiard balls under the bed.

The pool hall opened on Monday and was invaded by a hot-headed clientele. The billiard table had been covered with a purple cloth which gave the place a funereal air. A sign was tacked on the wall: "NO BALLS, NO BILLIARDS." People came in to read the sign as if it were news. Some stood before it for a long time, rereading it with impenetrable devotion.

Damaso was among the first customers. He had spent a part of his life on the benches set aside for the spectators, and he was there from the moment the doors opened. It was as difficult but as spontaneous as a condolence call. He gave the owner a pat on the back, from across the counter, and said:

"What a pain, Roque."

The owner shook his head with a pained little smile, sighing. "That's right," he said. And he continued waiting on the customers while Damaso, settled on one of the counter stools, regarded the ghostly table under its purple shroud.

"How strange," he said.

"That's right," agreed a man on the next stool. "It looks like we're in Holy Week."

When the majority of customers went to eat lunch, Damaso put a coin in the jukebox and picked a Mexican ballad whose position on the selector he knew by heart. Roque was moving tables and chairs to the back of the hall.

"What are you doing?" asked Damaso.

"I'm setting up for cards," replied Roque. "I have to do something until the balls come."

Moving almost hesitantly with a chair in each hand, he looked like a recent widower.

"When are they coming?" Damaso asked.

"Within a month, I hope."

"By then the others will have reappeared," said Damaso.

Roque observed the row of little tables with satisfaction. "They won't show up," he said, drying his forehead with his sleeve. "They've been starving the Negro since Saturday and he doesn't want to tell where they are." He measured Damaso through his glasses blurred with sweat.

"I'm sure he threw them into the river."

Damaso bit his lips.

"And the two hundred pesos?"

"Them either," said Roque. "They only found thirty on him."

They looked each other in the eye. Damaso could not have explained his impression that the look established between him and Roque a relationship of complicity. That afternoon, from the lavatory, Ana saw him come home dancing like a boxer. She followed him into the room.

"All settled," said Damaso. "The old man is so resigned that he ordered new balls. Now it's just a question of waiting until they all forget."

"And the Negro?"

"That's nothing," said Damaso, shrugging his shoulders. "If

they don't find the balls they'll have to let him go."

After the meal, they sat outside the front door and were talking to the neighbors until the loudspeaker at the movie went off. When they went to bed, Damaso was excited.

"A terrific job just occurred to me," he said.

Ana realized that he'd been mulling over the idea since dusk.

"I'll go from town to town," Damaso went on. "I'll steal the billiard balls in one and I'll sell them in the next. Every town has a pool hall."

"Until they shoot you."

"Shoot, what kind of shoot?" he said. "You only see that in the movies." Planted in the middle of the room, he was choking on his own enthusiasm. Ana began to get undressed, seemingly indifferent, but in reality listening to him with compassionate attention.

"I'm going to buy a row of suits," said Damaso, pointing with his forefinger at an imaginary closet the length of the wall. "From here to there. And also fifty pairs of shoes."

"God willing," said Ana.

Damaso fixed her with a serious look.

"You're not interested in my affairs," he said.

"They are very far away from me," said Ana. She put out the lamp, lay down next to the wall, and added with definite bitterness, "When you're thirty I'll be forty-seven."

"Don't be silly," said Damaso.

He felt his pockets for the matches. "You won't have to wrestle with any more clothes, either," he said, a little baffled. Ana gave him a light. She looked at the flame until the match went out, and threw it down. Stretched out in bed, Damaso kept talking.

"Do you know what billiard balls are made of?"

Ana didn't answer.

"Out of elephant tusks," he went on. "They are so hard to find that it takes a month for them to come. Can you imagine?"

"Go to sleep," interrupted Ana. "I have to get up at five."

Damaso had returned to his natural state. He spent the morning in bed smoking, and after the siesta he began to get ready to go out. At night he listened to the radio broadcast of the baseball championship in the pool hall. He had the ability to forget his projects with as much enthusiasm as he needed to think them up.

"Do you have any money?" he asked his wife on Saturday.

"Eleven pesos," she answered, adding softly, "It's the rent."

"I'll make a deal with you."

"What?"

"Lend them to me."

"We have to pay the rent."

"We'll pay it later."

Ana shook her head. Damaso grabbed her by the wrist and prevented her from getting up from the table where they had just eaten breakfast.

"It's just for a few days," he said, petting her arm with distracted tenderness. "When I sell the balls we'll have enough cash for everything."

Ana didn't yield.

That night Damaso took her to the movie and didn't take his hand off her shoulder even while he was talking with his friends during intermission. They saw snatches of the movie. When it was over, Damaso was impatient.

"Then I'll have to rob the money," he said.

Ana shrugged her shoulders. "I'll club the first person I find," said Damaso, pushing her through the crowd leaving the movie. "Then they'll take me to jail for murder." Ana smiled inwardly. But she remained firm. The following morning, after a stormy night, Damaso got dressed with visible and ominous haste. He passed close to his wife and growled:

"I'm never coming back."

Ana could not hold back a slight tremor.

"Have a good trip!" she shouted.

After he slammed the door, an empty and endless Sunday began for Damaso. The shiny crockery in the public market, and the brightly dressed women who, with their children, were leaving eight-o'clock Mass, lent a happy note to the plaza, but the air was beginning to stiffen with heat.

He spent the day in the pool hall. A group of men played cards in the morning, and before lunch there was a brief rush of customers. But it was obvious that the establishment had lost its attractiveness. Only at dusk, when the baseball program went on, did it recover a little of its old animation.

After they closed the hall, Damaso found himself with no place to go, in the plaza which now seemed drained. He went down the street parallel to the harbor, following the sound of some happy, distant music. At the end of the street there was an enormous, empty dance hall, decked out in faded paper garlands, and at the back of the hall a band on a wooden platform. A suffocating smell of makeup floated within.

Damaso sat at the counter. When the piece ended, the boy who played the cymbals in the band collected coins among the men who had been dancing. A girl left her partner in the middle of the floor and approached Damaso.

"What's new, Valentino?"

Damaso offered her a seat beside him. The bartender, face powdered and with a carnation on his ear, asked in falsetto:

"What will you have?"

The girl turned toward Damaso.

"What are we drinking?"

"Nothing."

"It's my treat."

"That's not it," said Damaso. "I'm hungry."

"Pity," sighed the bartender. "With those eyes."

They went into the dining room at the back of the hall. By the shape of her body, the girl seemed too young, but the crust of powder and rouge, and the lipstick on her lips, made it hard to know her real age. After they ate, Damaso followed her to the room at the back of a dark patio where they could hear the breathing of sleeping animals. The bed was occupied by an infant covered with colored rags. The girl put the rags in a wooden box, laid the infant inside, and then put the box on the floor.

"The mice will eat him," said Damaso.

"No, they don't," she said.

She changed her red dress for another with a lower neckline, with big yellow flowers.

"Who is the father?" Damaso asked.

"I haven't the slightest idea," she said. And then, from the doorway, "I'll be right back."

He heard her lock the door. He smoked several cigarettes, stretched out on his back and with his clothes on. The bedsprings vibrated in time to the bass drum. He didn't know at what point he fell asleep. When he awoke, the room seemed bigger in the music's absence.

The girl was getting undressed beside the bed.

"What time is it?"

"Around four," she said. "Did the child cry?"

"I don't think so," said Damaso.

The girl lay down very close to him, scrutinizing him with her eyes turned slightly away while she unbuttoned his shirt. Damaso realized that she had been drinking heavily. He tried to put out the light.

"Leave it on," she said. "I love to look in your eyes."

From dawn on, the room filled with rural noises. The child cried. The girl took him into bed and nursed him, humming a three-note song, until they all fell asleep. Damaso didn't notice that the girl woke up around seven, left the room, and came back without the child.

"Everybody is going down to the harbor," she said.

Damaso felt as if he hadn't slept more than an hour the whole night.

"What for?"

"To see the Negro who stole the balls," she said. "They're taking him away today."

Damaso lit a cigarette.

"Poor man." The girl sighed.

"Why poor?" said Damaso. "Nobody made him into a thief."

The girl thought for a moment with her head on his chest. In a very low voice she said:

"It wasn't him."

"Who said?"

"I know it," she said. "The night they broke into the pool hall, the Negro was with Gloria, and he spent the whole next day in her room, until around nighttime. Then they came to say they had arrested him in the movie."

"Gloria can tell the police."

"The Negro told them that," she said. "The Mayor went to Gloria's, turned the room upside down, and said he was going to take her to jail as an accomplice. Finally, it was settled for twenty pesos."

Damaso got up before eight.

"Stay here," the girl said. "I'm going to kill a chicken for lunch."

Damaso shook the comb into the palm of his hand before putting it in his back pocket. "I can't," he said, drawing the girl to him by the wrists. She had washed her face, and she was really very young, with two big black eyes which gave her a helpless look. She held him around the waist.

"Stay here," she insisted.

"Forever?"

She blushed slightly and drew back.

"Joker," she said.

Ana was exhausted that morning. But the town's excitement was contagious. Faster than usual, she collected the clothing to wash that week, and went to the harbor to witness the departure of the Negro. An impatient crowd was waiting next to the launches which were ready to shove off. Damaso was there.

Ana prodded him in the kidneys with her forefingers.

"What are you doing here?" asked Damaso, startled.

"I came to see you off," said Ana.

Damaso rapped on a lamppost with his knuckles.

"Damn you," he said.

After lighting a cigarette, he threw the empty pack into the river. Ana took another out of her chemise and put it in his shirt pocket. Damaso smiled for the first time.

"You never learn," he said.

Ana went "Ha, ha."

A little later they put the Negro on board. The took him through the middle of the plaza, his wrists tied behind his back with a rope held by a policeman. Two other policemen armed with rifles walked beside him. He was shirtless, his lower lip split open, and one eyebrow swollen, like a boxer. He avoided the crowd's looks with passive dignity. At the door of the pool hall, where the greater part of the crowd had gathered to witness both ends of the show, the owner watched him pass moving his head silently. The rest observed him with a sort of eagerness.

The launch cast off at once. The Negro was on deck, tied

hand and foot to an oil drum. When the launch turned around in the middle of the river and whistled for the last time, the Negro's back shone.

"Poor man," whispered Ana.

"Criminals," someone near her said. "A human being can't stand so much sun."

Damaso located the voice coming from an extraordinarily fat woman, and he began to move toward the plaza. "You talk too much," he hissed in Ana's ear. "Now all you have to do is to shout the whole story." She accompanied him to the door of the pool hall.

"At least go home and change," she said when she left him. "You look like a beggar."

The event had brought an excited group to the hall. Trying to serve them all, Roque was waiting on several tables at once. Damaso waited until he passed next to him.

"Would you like some help?"

Roque put half a dozen bottles of beer in front of him with glasses upended on the necks.

"Thanks, son."

Damaso took the bottles to the tables. He took several orders, and kept on taking and bringing bottles until the customers left for lunch. Early in the morning, when he returned to the room, Ana realized that he had been drinking. She took his hand and put it on her belly.

"Feel here," she said. "Don't you feel it?"

Damaso gave no sign of enthusiasm.

"He's kicking now," said Ana. "He spends all night giving me little kicks inside."

But he didn't react. Concentrating on himself, he went out very early the next day and didn't return until midnight. A week passed that way. For the few moments he spent in the house, smoking in bed, he avoided conversation. Ana intensified her attentions. On one particular occasion, at the beginning of their life together, he had behaved in the same way, and then she had not known him well enough not to bother him. Astride her in bed, Damaso had punched her and made her bleed.

This time she waited. At night she put a pack of cigarettes next to the lamp, knowing that he could stand hunger and thirst but not the need to smoke. At last, in the middle of July, Damaso returned to the room at dusk. Ana became nervous, thinking that he must be very confused to come looking for her at that hour. They ate in silence. But before going to bed Damaso was dazed and gentle, and out of the blue he said:

"I want to leave."

"Where to?"

"Anywhere."

Ana looked around the room. The magazine covers which she herself had cut out and pasted to the walls until they were completely covered with pictures of movie stars were faded and colorless. She had lost count of the men who, from being looked at so much from the bed, had disappeared gradually and taken those colors with them.

"You're bored with me," she said.

"It's not that," said Damaso. "It's this town."

"It's like every other town."

"I can't sell the balls," said Damaso.

"Leave the balls alone," said Ana. "As long as God gives me the strength to wrestle with the laundry you won't have to go around taking chances." And after a pause she added softly:

"I don't know how that business ever occurred to you."

Damaso finished his cigarette before speaking.

"It was so easy that I can't understand how it never occurred to anyone else," he said.

"For the money," admitted Ana. "But no one would have been stupid enough to steal the balls."

"I did it without thinking," Damaso said. "I was leaving when I saw them behind the counter in their little box, and I thought that it was all too much work to come away empty-handed."

"That was your mistake," said Ana.

Damaso felt relieved. "And meanwhile the new ones haven't come," he said. "They sent word that now they're more expensive, and Roque said he canceled the order." He lit another cigarette, and while he spoke, he felt that his heart was being freed from some dark preoccupation.

He told her that the owner had decided to sell the pool table. It wasn't worth much. The cloth, torn by the clumsy tricks of learners, had been repaired with different-colored squares and the whole piece needed to be replaced. Meanwhile the hall's customers, who had grown old with billiards, now had no other amusement than the broadcasts of the baseball championship.

"So," Damaso finished, "without wanting to, we hurt the whole town."

"For nothing," said Ana.

"Next week the championship is over," said Damaso.

"And that's not the worst of it," said Ana. "The worst is the Negro."

Lying against his shoulder, as in the early days, she knew what her husband was thinking. She waited until he finished the cigarette. Then, with a cautious voice, she said:

"Damaso."

"What's the matter?"

"Return them."

He lit another cigarette.

"That's what I've been thinking for days," he said. "But the bitch of it is that I can't figure out how."

So they decided to leave the balls in a public place. Then

Ana thought that while that would solve the problem of the pool hall, it would leave the problem of the Negro unsettled. The police could interpret the find in many ways, without absolving him. Nor did she forget the possibility that the balls might be found by someone who, instead of returning them, would keep them to sell them.

"Well, as long as the thing is going to be done," concluded Ana, "it's better to do it right."

They dug up the balls. Ana wrapped them in newspapers, taking care that the wrapping should not reveal the shape of the contents, and she put them in the trunk.

"We have to wait for the right occasion," she said.

But they spent weeks waiting for the right occasion. The night of August 20th—two months after the robbery—Damaso found Roque seated behind the counter, shooing the mosquitoes away with a fan. With the radio off, his loneliness seemed more intense.

"I told you," Roque exclaimed with a certain joy at the prediction come true. "Business has gone to hell."

Damaso put a coin in the jukebox. The volume of the music and the machine's play of colors seemed to him a noisy proof of his loyalty. But he had the impression that Roque didn't notice it. Then he pulled up a seat and tried to console him with confused arguments which the proprietor demolished emotionlessly, to the careless rhythm of his fan.

"Nothing can be done about it," he was saying. "The baseball championship couldn't last forever."

"But the balls may show up."

"They won't show up."

"The Negro couldn't have eaten them."

"The police looked everywhere," said Roque with an exasperating certainty. "He threw them into the river."

"A miracle could happen."

"Forget your illusions, son," replied Roque. "Misfortune is like a snail. Do you believe in miracles?"

"Sometimes," said Damaso.

When he left the place, the movie hadn't yet ended. The loudspeaker's lengthy and broken dialogues resounded in the darkened town, and there was something temporary in the few houses which were still open. Damaso wandered a moment in the direction of the movie. Then he went to the dance hall.

The band was playing for a lone customer who was dancing with two women at once. The others, judiciously seated against the wall, seemed to be waiting for the mail. Damaso sat down at a table, made a sign to the bartender to bring him a beer, and drank it from the bottle with brief pauses to breathe, observing as if through a glass the man who was dancing with the two women. He was shorter than they were.

At midnight the women who had been at the movies arrived, pursued by a group of men. Damaso's friend, who was with them, left the others and sat at his table.

Damaso didn't look at her. He had drunk half a dozen beers and kept staring at the man, who now was dancing with three women but without paying attention to them, diverted by the intricate movements of his own feet. He looked happy, and it was evident that he would have been even happier if, in addition to his legs and arms, he had had a tail.

"I don't like that guy," said Damaso.

"Then don't look at him," said the girl.

She ordered a drink from the bartender. The dance floor began to fill up with couples, but the man with the three women kept on as if he were alone in the hall. On one turn his eyes met Damaso's and he pressed an even greater effort into his dancing, and showed him a smile with his rabbit's teeth. Damaso stood his look without blinking, until the man got serious and turned his back.

"He thinks he's very happy," said Damaso.

"He is very happy," said the girl. "Every time he comes to town, he picks up the bill for the music, like all the traveling salesmen."

Damaso averted his eyes, turning them on her.

"Then go with him," he said. "Where there's enough for three, there's enough for four."

Without replying she turned her face toward the dance floor, drinking with slow sips. The pale-yellow dress accented her shyness.

They danced the next set. When it was over, Damaso was smoldering. "I'm dying of hunger," the girl said, leading him by the arm toward the counter. "You have to eat, too." The happy man was coming in the opposite direction with the three women.

"Listen," Damaso said to him.

The man smiled at him without stopping. Damaso let go of his companion's arm and blocked his path.

"I don't like your teeth."

The man blanched, but kept smiling.

"Me neither," he said.

Before the girl could stop it, Damaso punched him in the face and the man sat down in the middle of the dance floor. None of the customers interfered. The three women hugged Damaso around the waist, shouting, while his companion pushed him toward the back of the hall. The man got up, his face out of joint from the blow. He jumped like a monkey to the center of the dance floor and shouted:

"On with the music!"

Toward two o'clock the hall was almost empty, and the women without customers began to eat. It was hot. The girl brought a dish of rice with beans and fried meat to the table, and ate it all with a spoon. Damaso watched her in a sort of stupor. She held out a spoonful of rice to him.

"Open your mouth."

Damaso lowered his chin to his chest and shook his head. "That's for women," he said. "We men don't eat."

He had to rest his hands on the table in order to stand up. When he regained his balance, the bartender was in front of him, arms crossed.

"It comes to nine-eighty," he said. "This party's not on the house."

Damaso pushed him aside.

"I don't like queers," he said.

The bartender grabbed him by the sleeve but, at a sign from the girl, let him pass, saying:

"You don't know what you're missing."

Damaso stumbled outside. The mysterious sheen of the river beneath the moon opened a furrow of lucidity in his brain. But it closed immediately. When he saw the door to his room, on the other side of town, Damaso was certain that he had walked in his sleep. He shook his head. In a confused but urgent way he realized that from that moment on he had to watch every one of his movements. He pushed the door carefully to keep the hinges from creaking.

Ana felt him looking in the trunk. She turned toward the wall to avoid the light from the lamp, but then realized that her husband was not getting undressed. A flash of intuition made her sit up in bed. Damaso was next to the trunk, with the package of balls and the flashlight in his hand.

He put his forefinger on his lips.

Ana jumped out of bed. "You're crazy," she murmured, running toward the door. She shot the bolt quickly. Damaso put the flashlight in his pants pocket, together with the little knife and some sharpened files, and advanced toward her gripping the package under his arm. Ana leaned her back against the door.

"You won't leave here as long as I'm alive," she said quietly.

Damaso tried to push her aside. "Get away," he said. Ana

grabbed the doorjamb with both hands. They looked each other in the eye without blinking. "You're an ass," whispered Ana. "What God gave you in your looks he took away from your brains." Damaso grabbed her by the hair, twisted her wrist, and made her lower her head; with clenched teeth he said, "I told you get away." Ana looked at him out of the corner of her eye, like an ox under the yoke. For a moment she felt invulnerable to pain and stronger than her husband, but he kept twisting her hair until her tears choked her.

"You're going to kill the baby in my belly," she said.

Damaso dragged, almost carried, her bodily to the bed. When he let her go, she jumped on his back, wrapped her legs and arms around him, and both of them fell on the bed. They had begun to get winded. "I'll scream," Ana whispered in his ear. "If you move I'll scream." Damaso snorted in rage, hitting her knees with the package of balls. Ana let out a cry and loosened her legs, but fastened herself to his waist to prevent him from reaching the door. Then she began to beg. "I promise you I'll take them tomorrow myself," she was saying. "I'll put them back so no one will notice." Nearer and nearer to the door, Damaso was hitting her hands with the balls. She would let him go for a moment to get over the pain. Then she would grab him again, and continue begging.

"I can say it was me," she was saying. "They can't put me in jail in my condition."

Damaso shook her off. "The whole town will see you," Ana said. "You're so dumb you don't realize there's a full moon." She grabbed him again before he got the bolt open. Then, with closed eyes, she pummeled him in the neck and face, almost shouting, "Animal, animal." Damaso tried to ward off the blows and she clutched the bolt and took it out of his hands. She threw a blow at his head. Damaso dodged it, and the bolt resounded on his shoulder bone as on a pane of glass.

"Bitch!" he shouted.

At that moment he wasn't concerned about not making noise. He hit her on the ear with the back of his fist, and felt the deep cry and heavy impact of her body against the wall, but he didn't look at her. He left the room without closing the door.

Ana stayed on the floor, stupefied by the pain, and waited for something to happen in her abdomen. They called her from the other side of the wall in a voice which sounded as if it came from beyond the grave. She bit her lips to keep from crying. Then she got up and got dressed. It did not occur to her—as it had not the first time—that Damaso might still be outside the room, telling himself that the plan had failed and waiting for her to come outside shouting. She made the same mistake a second time: instead of pursuing her husband, she put on her shoes, closed the door, and sat down on the bed to wait.

Only when the door closed did Damaso understand that he couldn't go back. The clamor of dogs pursued him to the end of the street, but then there was a ghostly silence. He avoided the sidewalks, trying to escape his own steps, which sounded huge and alien in the sleeping town. He took no precautions until he was in the empty lot at the rear door of the pool hall.

This time he didn't have to make use of the flashlight. The door had been reinforced only at the point of the broken staple. They had taken out a piece of wood the size and shape of a brick, replaced it with new wood, and put the same staple back again. The rest was the same. Damaso pulled on the lock with his left hand, put the end of a file between the legs of the staple that had not been reinforced, and moved the file back and forth like a gearshift lever, with force but without violence, until the wood gave way in a plaintive explosion of rotted splinters. Before he pushed the door, he raised it into line to lessen the noise of its scraping on the bricks of the floor. He opened it just halfway. Finally he took off his shoes, slid them inside with the package of balls, and, crossing himself, entered the room flooded in moonlight.

Right in front of him there was a dark passageway crammed with bottles and empty boxes. Farther on, beneath the flood of light from the glass skylight, was the billiard table, and then the back of the cabinets, and finally the little tables and the chairs piled up against the back of the front door. Everything was the same as the first time, except the flood of moonlight and the crispness of the silence. Damaso, who until that moment had had to subdue his nervous system, felt a strange fascination.

This time he wasn't careful of the loose bricks. He blocked the door with his shoes and, after crossing the flood of light, lit the flashlight to look for the little box the balls belonged in behind the counter. He acted without caution. Moving the flashlight from left to right, he saw a pile of dusty jars, a pair of stirrups with spurs, a rolled-up shirt soiled with motor oil, and then the little box in the same spot where he had left it. But he didn't stop the beam of light until the end of the counter. There was the cat.

The animal looked at him without mystery, against the light. Damaso kept the light on him until he remembered with a slight shiver that he had never seen him in the place during the day. He moved the flash forward, saying, "Scat," but the animal remained impassive. Then there was a kind of silent detonation inside his head, and the cat disappeared completely from his memory. When he realized what was happening, he had already dropped the flashlight and was hugging the package of balls against his chest. The room was lit up.

"Well!"

He recognized Roque's voice. He stood up slowly, feeling a terrible fatigue in his kidneys. Roque approached from the rear of the room, in his underwear and with an iron bar in his hand, still dazzled by the brightness. There was a hammock hanging behind the bottles and the empty boxes, very near the spot Damaso had passed when he came in. This also was different from the first time.

When he was less than thirty feet away, Roque gave a little hop and got on his guard. Damaso hid the hand with the package behind him. Roque wrinkled his nose and thrust out his head, trying to recognize him without his glasses.

"You!" he exclaimed.

Damaso felt as if something infinite had ended at last. Roque lowered the bar and approached with his mouth open. Without glasses and without his false teeth, he looked like a woman.

"What are you doing here?"

"Nothing," said Damaso.

He changed his position with an imperceptible movement of his body.

"What do you have there?" asked Roque.

Damaso stepped back. "Nothing," he said. Roque reddened and began to tremble. "What do you have there!" he shouted, stepping forward with the bar raised. Damaso gave him the package. Roque took it with his left hand, still on guard, and examined it with his fingers. Only then did he understand.

"It can't be," he said.

He was so perplexed that he put the bar on the counter and seemed to forget Damaso while he was opening the package. He contemplated the balls silently.

"I came to put them back," said Damaso.

"Of course," said Roque.

Damaso felt limp. The alcohol had left him completely, and there was only a gravelly sediment left on his tongue, and a confused feeling of loneliness. "So that was the miracle," said Roque, wrapping up the package. "I can't believe you could be so stupid." When he raised his head, he had changed his expression.

"And the two hundred pesos?"

"There was nothing in the drawer," said Damaso.

Roque looked at him thoughtfully, chewing emptily, and then smiled. "There was nothing," he repeated several times. "So there was nothing." He grasped the bar again, saying:

"Well, we're going to tell the Mayor this story right now."

Damaso dried the sweat of his hands on his pants.

"You know there was nothing."

Roque kept smiling.

"There were two hundred pesos," he said. "And now they're going to take them out of your hide, not so much for being a thief as for being a fool."

BALTHAZAR'S
MARVELOUS AFTERNOON

THE CAGE was finished. Balthazar hung it under the eave, from force of habit, and when he finished lunch everyone was already saying that it was the most beautiful cage in the world. So many people came to see it that a crowd formed in front of the house, and Balthazar had to take it down and close the shop.

"You have to shave," Ursula, his wife, told him. "You look like a Capuchin."

"It's bad to shave after lunch," said Balthazar.

He had two weeks' growth, short, hard, and bristly hair like the mane of a mule, and the general expression of a frightened boy. But it was a false expression. In February he was thirty; he had been living with Ursula for four years, without marrying her and without having children, and life had given him many reasons to be on guard but none to be frightened. He did not even know that for some people the cage he had just made was the most beautiful one in the world. For him, accustomed to making cages since childhood, it had been hardly any more difficult than the others.

"Then rest for a while," said the woman. "With that beard you can't show yourself anywhere."

While he was resting, he had to get out of his hammock several times to show the cage to the neighbors. Ursula had paid little attention to it until then. She was annoyed because her husband had neglected the work of his carpenter's shop to devote himself entirely to the cage, and for two weeks had slept poorly, turning over and muttering incoherencies, and he hadn't thought of shaving. But her annoyance dissolved in the face of the finished cage. When Balthazar woke up from his nap, she had ironed his pants and a shirt; she had put them on a chair near the hammock and had carried the cage to the dining table. She regarded it in silence.

"How much will you charge?" she asked.

"I don't know," Balthazar answered. "I'm going to ask for thirty pesos to see if they'll give me twenty."

"Ask for fifty," said Ursula. "You've lost a lot of sleep in these two weeks. Furthermore, it's rather large. I think it's the biggest cage I've ever seen in my life."

Balthazar began to shave.

"Do you think they'll give me fifty pesos?"

"That's nothing for Mr. Chepe Montiel, and the cage is worth it," said Ursula. "You should ask for sixty."

The house lay in the stifling shadow. It was the first week of April and the heat seemed less bearable because of the chirping of the cicadas. When he finished dressing, Balthazar opened the door to the patio to cool off the house, and a group of children entered the dining room.

The news had spread. Dr. Octavio Giraldo, an old physician, happy with life but tired of his profession, thought about Balthazar's cage while he was eating lunch with his invalid wife. On the inside terrace, where they put the table on hot days, there were many flowerpots and two cages with canaries. His wife liked birds, and she liked them so much that she hated cats because they could eat them up. Thinking about her, Dr. Giraldo went to see a patient that afternoon, and when he returned he went by Balthazar's house to inspect the cage.

There were a lot of people in the dining room. The cage was on display on the table: with its enormous dome of wire, three stories inside, with passageways and compartments especially for eating and sleeping and swings in the space set aside for the birds' recreation, it seemed like a small-scale model of a gigantic ice factory. The doctor inspected it carefully, without touching it, thinking that in effect the cage was better than its reputation, and much more beautiful than any he had ever dreamed of for his wife.

"This is a flight of the imagination," he said. He sought out Balthazar among the group of people and, fixing his maternal eyes on him, added, "You would have been an extraordinary architect."

Balthazar blushed.

"Thank you," he said.

"It's true," said the doctor. He was smoothly and delicately fat, like a woman who had been beautiful in her youth, and he had delicate hands. His voice seemed like that of a priest speaking Latin. "You wouldn't even need to put birds in it," he said, making the cage turn in front of the audience's eyes as if he were auctioning it off. "It would be enough to hang it in the trees so it could sing by itself." He put it back on the table, thought a moment, looking at the cage, and said:

"Fine, then I'll take it."

"It's sold," said Ursula.

"It belongs to the son of Mr. Chepe Montiel," said Balthazar. "He ordered it specially."

The doctor adopted a respectful attitude.

"Did he give you the design?"

"No," said Balthazar. "He said he wanted a large cage, like this one, for a pair of troupials."

The doctor looked at the cage.

"But this isn't for troupials."

"Of course it is, Doctor," said Balthazar, approaching the table. The children surrounded him. "The measurements are carefully calculated," he said, pointing to the different compartments with his forefinger. Then he struck the dome with his knuckles, and the cage filled with resonant chords.

"It's the strongest wire you can find, and each joint is soldered outside and in," he said.

"It's even big enough for a parrot," interrupted one of the children.

"That it is," said Balthazar.

The doctor turned his head.

"Fine, but he didn't give you the design," he said. "He gave you no exact specifications, aside from making it a cage big enough for troupials. Isn't that right?"

"That's right," said Balthazar.

"Then there's no problem," said the doctor. "One thing is a cage big enough for troupials, and another is this cage. There's no proof that this one is the one you were asked to make."

"It's this very one," said Balthazar, confused. "That's why I made it."

The doctor made an impatient gesture.

"You could make another one," said Ursula, looking at her husband. And then, to the doctor: "You're not in any hurry."

"I promised it to my wife for this afternoon," said the doctor.

"I'm very sorry, Doctor," said Balthazar, "but I can't sell you something that's sold already."

The doctor shrugged his shoulders. Drying the sweat from his neck with a handkerchief, he contemplated the cage silently with the fixed, unfocused gaze of one who looks at a ship which is sailing away.

"How much did they pay you for it?"

Balthazar sought out Ursula's eyes without replying.

"Sixty pesos," she said.

The doctor kept looking at the cage. "It's very pretty." He sighed. "Extremely pretty." Then, moving toward the door, he began to fan himself energetically, smiling, and the trace of that episode disappeared forever from his memory.

"Montiel is very rich," he said.

In truth, José Montiel was not as rich as he seemed, but he would have been capable of doing anything to become so. A few blocks from there, in a house crammed with equipment, where no one had ever smelled a smell that couldn't be sold, he remained indifferent to the news of the cage. His wife, tortured by an obsession with death, closed the doors and windows after lunch and lay for two hours with her eyes opened to the shadow of the room, while José Montiel took his siesta. The clamor of many voices surprised her there. Then she opened the door to the living room and found a crowd in front of the house, and Balthazar with the cage in the middle of the crowd, dressed in white, freshly shaved, with that expression of decorous candor with which the poor approach the houses of the wealthy.

"What a marvelous thing!" José Montiel's wife exclaimed, with a radiant expression, leading Balthazar inside. "I've never seen anything like it in my life," she said, and added, annoyed by the crowd which piled up at the door:

"But bring it inside before they turn the living room into a grandstand."

Balthazar was no stranger to José Montiel's house. On different occasions, because of his skill and forthright way of dealing, he had been called in to do minor carpentry jobs. But he never felt at ease among the rich. He used to think about them, about their ugly and argumentative wives, about their tremendous surgical operations, and he always experienced a feeling of pity. When he entered their houses, he couldn't move without dragging his feet.

"Is Pepe home?" he asked.

He had put the cage on the dining-room table.

"He's at school," said José Montiel's wife. "But he shouldn't be long," and she added, "Montiel is taking a bath."

In reality, José Montiel had not had time to bathe. He was giving himself an urgent alcohol rub, in order to come out and see what was going on. He was such a cautious man that he slept without an electric fan so he could watch over the noises of the house while he slept.

"Adelaide!" he shouted. "What's going on?"

"Come and see what a marvelous thing!" his wife shouted.

José Montiel, obese and hairy, his towel draped around his neck, appeared at the bedroom window.

"What is that?"

"Pepe's cage," said Balthazar.

His wife looked at him perplexedly.

"Whose?"

"Pepe's," replied Balthazar. And then, turning toward José Montiel, "Pepe ordered it."

Nothing happened at that instant, but Balthazar felt as if someone had just opened the bathroom door on him. José Montiel came out of the bedroom in his underwear.

"Pepe!" he shouted.

"He's not back," whispered his wife, motionless.

Pepe appeared in the doorway. He was about twelve, and had the same curved eyelashes and was as quietly pathetic as his mother.

"Come here," José Montiel said to him. "Did you order this?"

The child lowered his head. Grabbing him by the hair, José Montiel forced Pepe to look him in the eye.

"Answer me."

The child bit his lip without replying.

"Montiel," whispered his wife.

José Montiel let the child go and turned toward Balthazar in a fury. "I'm very sorry, Balthazar," he said. "But you should have consulted me before going on. Only to you would it occur to contract with a minor." As he spoke, his face recovered its serenity. He lifted the cage without looking at it and gave it to Balthazar.

"Take it away at once, and try to sell it to whomever you can," he said. "Above all, I beg you not to argue with me." He patted him on the back and explained, "The doctor has forbidden me to get angry."

The child had remained motionless, without blinking, until Balthazar looked at him uncertainly with the cage in his hand. Then he emitted a guttural sound, like a dog's growl, and threw himself on the floor screaming.

José Montiel looked at him, unmoved, while the mother tried to pacify him. "Don't even pick him up," he said. "Let him break his head on the floor, and then put salt and lemon on it so he can rage to his heart's content." The child was shrieking tearlessly while his mother held him by the wrists.

"Leave him alone," José Montiel insisted.

Balthazar observed the child as he would have observed the death throes of a rabid animal. It was almost four o'clock. At that hour, at his house, Ursula was singing a very old song and cutting slices of onion.

"Pepe," said Balthazar.

He approached the child, smiling, and held the cage out to him. The child jumped up, embraced the cage which was almost as big as he was, and stood looking at Balthazar through the wirework without knowing what to say. He hadn't shed one tear.

"Balthazar," said José Montiel softly. "I told you already to take it away."

"Give it back," the woman ordered the child.

"Keep it," said Balthazar. And then, to José Montiel: "After all, that's what I made it for."

José Montiel followed him into the living room.

"Don't be foolish, Balthazar," he was saying, blocking his path. "Take your piece of furniture home and don't be silly. I have no intention of paying you a cent."

"It doesn't matter," said Balthazar. "I made it expressly as a gift for Pepe. I didn't expect to charge anything for it."

As Balthazar made his way through the spectators who were blocking the door, José Montiel was shouting in the middle of the living room. He was very pale and his eyes were beginning to get red.

"Idiot!" he was shouting. "Take your trinket out of here. The last thing we need is for some nobody to give orders in my house. Son of a bitch!"

In the pool hall, Balthazar was received with an ovation. Until that moment, he thought that he had made a better cage than ever before, that he'd had to give it to the son of José Montiel so he wouldn't keep crying, and that none of these things was particularly important. But then he realized that all of this had a certain importance for many people, and he felt a little excited.

"So they gave you fifty pesos for the cage."

"Sixty," said Balthazar.

"Score one for you," someone said. "You're the only one who has managed to get such a pile of money out of Mr. Chepe Montiel. We have to celebrate."

They bought him a beer, and Balthazar responded with a round for everybody. Since it was the first time he had ever been out drinking, by dusk he was completely drunk, and he was talking about a fabulous project of a thousand cages, at sixty pesos each, and then of a million cages, till he had sixty million pesos. "We have to make a lot of things to sell to the rich before they die," he was saying, blind drunk. "All of them are sick, and they're going to die. They're so screwed up they can't even get angry any more." For two hours he was paying for the jukebox, which played without interruption. Everybody toasted Balthazar's health, good luck, and fortune, and the death of the rich, but at mealtime they left him alone in the pool hall.

Ursula had waited for him until eight, with a dish of fried meat covered with slices of onion. Someone told her that her husband was in the pool hall, delirious with happiness, buying beers for everyone, but she didn't believe it, because Balthazar had never got drunk. When she went to bed, almost at midnight, Balthazar was in a lighted room where there were little tables, each with four chairs, and an outdoor dance floor, where the plovers were walking around. His face was smeared with rouge, and since he couldn't take one more step, he thought he wanted to lie down with two women in the same bed. He had spent so much that he had had to leave his watch in pawn, with the promise to pay the next day. A moment later, spread-eagled in the street, he realized that his shoes were being taken off, but he didn't want to abandon the happiest dream of his life. The women who passed on their way to five-o'clock Mass didn't dare look at him, thinking he was dead.

MONTIEL'S WIDOW

WHEN JOSÉ MONTIEL died, everyone felt avenged except his widow; but it took several hours for everyone to believe that he had indeed died. Many continued to doubt it after seeing the corpse in the sweltering room, crammed along with pillows and linen sheets into a yellow coffin, with sides as rounded as a melon. He was very closely shaved, dressed in white, with patent-leather boots, and he looked so well that he had never seemed as alive as at that moment. It was the same Mr. Chepe Montiel as was present every Sunday at eight-o'clock Mass, except that instead of his riding quirt he had a crucifix in his hands. It took screwing the lid on the coffin and walling him up in the showy family mausoleum for the whole town to become convinced that he wasn't playing dead.

After the burial, the only thing which seemed incredible to everyone except his widow was that José Montiel had died a natural death. While everyone had been hoping he would be shot in the back in an ambush, his widow was certain she would see him die an old man in his bed, having confessed, and painlessly, like a modern-day saint. She was mistaken in only a few details. José Montiel died in his hammock, the second of August, 1951, at two in the afternoon, as a result of a fit of anger which the doctor had forbidden. But his wife also was hoping that the whole town would attend the funeral and that the house would be too small to hold all the flowers. Nevertheless only the members of his own party and of his religious brotherhood attended, and the only wreaths they received were those from the municipal government. His son, from his consular post in Germany, and his two daughters, from Paris, sent three-page telegrams. One could see that they had written them standing up, with the plentiful ink of the telegraph office, and that they had torn up many telegram forms before finding twenty dollars' worth of words. None of them promised to come back. That night, at the age of sixty-two, while crying on the pillow upon which the head of the man who had made her happy had rested, the widow of Montiel knew for the first time the taste of resentment. I'll lock myself up forever, she was thinking. For me, it is as if they had put me in the same box as José Montiel. I don't want to know anything more about this world.

She was sincere, that fragile woman, lacerated by superstition, married at twenty by her parents' will to the only suitor they had allowed her to see at less than thirty feet; she had never been in direct contact with reality. Three days after they took her husband's body out of the house, she understood through her tears that she ought to pull herself together, but she could not find the direction of her new life. She had to begin at the beginning.

Among the innumerable secrets José Montiel had taken with him to the grave was the combination of the safe. The Mayor took on the problem. He ordered the safe put in the patio, against the wall, and two policemen fired their rifles at the lock. All morning long the widow heard from the bedroom the muffled reports successively ordered by the Mayor's shouts.

That's the last straw, she thought. Five years spent praying to God to end the shooting, and now I have to thank them for shooting in my house.

That day, she made a concerted effort to summon death, but no one replied. She was beginning to fall asleep when a tremendous explosion shook the foundations of the house. They had had to dynamite the safe.

Montiel's widow heaved a sigh. October was interminable with its swampy rains, and she felt lost, sailing without direction in the chaotic and fabulous hacienda of José Montiel.

Mr. Carmichael, an old and diligent friend of the family, had taken charge of the estate. When at last she faced the concrete fact that her husband had died, Montiel's widow came out of the bedroom to take care of the house. She stripped it of all decoration, had the furniture covered in mourning colors, and put funeral ribbons on the portraits of the dead man which hung on the walls. In the two months after the funeral, she had acquired the habit of biting her nails. One day—her eyes reddened and swollen from crying so much—she realized that Mr. Carmichael was entering the house with an open umbrella.

"Close that umbrella, Mr. Carmichael," she told him. "After all the misfortune we've had, all we need is for you to come into the house with your umbrella open."

Mr. Carmichael put the umbrella in the corner. He was an old Negro, with shiny skin, dressed in white, and with little slits made with a knife in his shoes to relieve the pressure of his bunions.

"It's only while it's drying."

For the first time since her husband died, the widow opened the window.

"So much misfortune and, in addition, this winter," she murmured, biting her nails. "It seems as though it will never clear up."

"It won't clear up today or tomorrow," said the executor. "Last night my bunions wouldn't let me sleep."

She trusted the atmospheric predictions of Mr. Carmichael's bunions. She contemplated the desolate little plaza, the silent houses whose doors did not open to witness the funeral of José Montiel, and then she felt desperate, with her nails, with her limitless lands, and with the infinite number of obligations which she inherited from her husband and which she would never manage to understand.

"The world is all wrong," she said, sobbing.

Those who visited her in those days had many reasons to think she had gone mad. But she was never more lucid than then. Since before the political slaughter began, she had spent the sad October mornings in front of the window in her room, sympathizing with the dead and thinking that if God had not rested on Sunday He would have had time to finish the world properly. "He should have used that day to tie up a few of the loose ends," she used to say. "After all, He had all eternity to rest." The only difference, after the death of her husband, was that then she had a concrete reason for harboring such dark thoughts.

Thus, while Montiel's widow ate herself up in desperation, Mr. Carmichael tried to prevent the shipwreck. Things weren't going well. Free of the threat of José Montiel, who had monopolized local business through terror, the town was taking reprisals. Waiting for customers who never came, the milk went sour in the jugs lined up in the patio, and the honey spoiled in its combs, and the cheese fattened worms in the dark cabinets of the cheesehouse. In his mausoleum adorned with electric-light bulbs and imitation-marble archangels, José Montiel was paying for six years of murders and oppression. No one in the history of the country had got so rich in so short a time. When the first Mayor of the dictatorship arrived in town, José Montiel was a discreet partisan of all regimes who had spent half his life in his underwear seated in front of his rice mill. At one time he enjoyed a certain reputation as a lucky man, and a good believer, because he promised out loud to give the Church a life-size image of Saint Joseph if he won the lottery, and two weeks later he won himself a fat prize and kept his promise. The first time he was seen to wear shoes was when the new Mayor, a brutish, underhanded police sergeant, arrived with express orders to liquidate the opposition. José Montiel began by being his confidential informer. That modest businessman, whose fat man's quiet humor never awakened the least uneasiness, segregated his enemies into rich and poor. The police shot down the poor in the public square. The rich were given a period of twenty-four hours to get out of town. Planning the massacre, José Montiel was closeted together with the Mayor in his stifling office for days on end, while his wife was sympathizing with the dead. When the Mayor left the office, she would block her husband's ways. "That man is a murderer," she would tell him. "Use your influence with the government to get them to take that beast away; he's not going to leave a single human being in town alive." And José Montiel, so busy those days, put her aside without looking at her, saying, "Don't be such a fool." In reality, his business was not the killing of the poor but the expulsion of the rich. After the Mayor riddled their doors with gunfire and gave them their twenty-four hours to get out of town, José Montiel bought their lands and cattle from them for a price which he himself set. "Don't be silly," his wife told him. You'll ruin yourself helping them so that they won't die of hunger someplace else, and they will never thank you." And José Montiel, who now didn't even have time to smile, brushed her aside, saying, "Go to your kitchen and don't bother me so much." At this rate, in less than a year the opposition was liquidated, and José Montiel was the richest and most powerful man in town. He sent his daughters to Paris, found a consular post in Germany for his son, and devoted himself to consolidating his empire. But he didn't live to enjoy even six years of his outrageous wealth.

After the first anniversary of his death, the widow heard the stairs creak only with the arrival of bad news. Someone always came at dusk. "Again the bandits," they used to say. "Yesterday they made off with a herd of fifty heifers." Motionless in her rocker, biting her nails, Montiel's widow fed on nothing but resentment.

"I told you, José Montiel," she was saying, talking to herself. "This is an unappreciative town. You are still warm in your grave, and already everyone has turned their backs on us."

No one came to the house again. The only human being whom she saw in those interminable months when it did not stop raining was the persistent Mr. Carmichael, who never entered the house with his umbrella closed. Things were going no better. Mr. Carmichael had written several letters to José Montiel's son. He suggested that it would be convenient if he came to take charge of affairs, and he even allowed himself to make some personal observations about the health of the widow. He always received evasive answers. At last, the son of José Montiel replied that frankly he didn't dare return for fear he would be shot. Then Mr. Carmichael went up to the widow's bedroom and had to confess to her that she was ruined.

"Better that way," she said. "I'm up to here with cheese and flies. If you want, take what you need and let me die in peace."

Her only contacts with the world, from then on, were the letters which she wrote her daughters at the end of every month. "This is a blighted town," she told them. "Stay there forever, and don't worry about me. I am happy knowing that you are happy." Her daughters took turns answering her. Their letters were always happy, and one could see that they had been written in warm, well-lit places, and that the girls saw themselves reflected in many mirrors when they stopped to think. They didn't wish to return either. "This is civilization," they would say. "There, on the other hand, it's not a good atmosphere for us. It's impossible to live in a country so savage that people are killed for political reasons." Reading the letters, Montiel's widow felt better, and she nodded her head in agreement at every phrase.

On a certain occasion, her daughters wrote her about the butcher shops of Paris. They told her about the pink pigs that were killed there and then hung up whole in the doorways, decorated with wreaths and garlands of flowers. At the end of the letter, a hand different from her daughters' had added, "Imagine! They put the biggest and prettiest carnation in the pig's ass."

Reading that phrase, for the first time in two years Montiel's widow smiled. She went up to her bedroom without turning out the lights in the house and, before lying down, turned the electric fan over against the wall. Then, from the night-table drawer she took some scissors, a can of Band-Aids, and a rosary, and she bandaged the nail of her right thumb, which was irritated by her biting. Then she began to pray, but at the second mystery she put the rosary into her left hand, because she couldn't feel the beads through the bandage. For a moment she heard the vibration of distant thunder. Then she fell asleep with her head bent on her breast. The hand with the rosary fell to her side, and then she saw Big Mama in the patio, with a white sheet and a comb in her lap, squashing lice with her thumbnails. She asked her:

"When am I going to die?"

Big Mama raised her head.

"When the tiredness begins in your arm."

ONE DAY
AFTER SATURDAY

THE TROUBLE began in July, when Rebecca, an embittered widow who lived in an immense house with two galleries and nine bedrooms, discovered that the screens were torn as if they had been stoned from the street. She made the first discovery in her bedroom and thought that she must speak to Argenida, her servant and confidante since her husband died. Later, moving things around (for a long time Rebecca had done nothing but move things around), she noticed that not only the screens in her bedroom but those in all the rest of the house were torn, too. The widow had an academic sense of authority, inherited perhaps from her paternal great-grandfather, a creole who in the War of Independence had fought on the side of the Royalists and later made an arduous journey to Spain with the sole purpose of visiting the palace which Charles III built in San Ildefonso. So that when she discovered the state of the other screens, she thought no more about speaking to Argenida about it but, rather, put on her straw hat with the tiny velvet flowers and went to the town hall to make a report about the attack. But when she got there, she saw that the Mayor himself, shirtless, hairy, and with a solidity which seemed bestial to her, was busy repairing the town hall screens, torn like her own.

Rebecca burst into the dirty and cluttered office, and the first thing she saw was a pile of dead birds on the desk. But she was disconcerted, in part by the heat and in part by the indignation which the destruction of her screens had produced in her, so that she did not have time to shudder at the unheard-of spectacle of the dead birds on the desk. Nor was she scandalized by the evidence of authority degraded, at the top of a stairway, repairing the metal threads of the window with a roll of screening and a screwdriver. She was not thinking now of any other dignity than her own, mocked by her own screens, and her absorption prevented her even from connecting the windows of her house with those of the town hall. She planted herself with discreet solemnity two steps inside the door and, leaning on the long ornate handle of her parasol, said:

"I have to register a complaint."

From the top of the stairway, the Mayor turned his head, flushed from the heat. He showed no emotion before the gratuitous presence of the widow in his office. With gloomy nonchalance he continued untacking the ruined screen, and asked from up above:

"What is the trouble?"

"The boys from the neighborhood broke my screens."

The Mayor took another look at her. He examined her carefully, from the elegant little velvet flowers to her shoes the color of old silver, and it was as if he were seeing her for the first time in his life. He descended with great economy of movement, without taking his eyes off her, and when he reached the bottom, he rested one hand on his belt, motioned with the screwdriver toward the desk, and said:

"It's not the boys, Señora. It's the birds."

And it was then that she connected the dead birds on the desk with the man at the top of the stairs, and with the broken screens of her bedrooms. She shuddered, imagining all the bedrooms in her house full of dead birds.

"The birds!" she exclaimed.

"The birds," the Mayor concurred. "It's strange you haven't noticed, since we've had this problem with the birds breaking windows and dying inside the houses for three days."

When she left the town hall, Rebecca felt ashamed. And a little resentful of Argenida, who dragged all the town gossip into her house and who nevertheless had not spoken to her about the birds. She opened her parasol, dazzled by the brightness of an impending August, and while she walked along the stifling and deserted street she had the impression that the bedrooms of all the houses were giving off a strong and penetrating stench of dead birds.

This was at the end of July, and never in the history of the town had it been so hot. But the inhabitants, alarmed by the death of the birds, did not notice that. Even though the strange phenomenon had not seriously affected the town's activities, the majority were held in suspense by it at the beginning of August. A majority among whom was not numbered His Reverence, Anthony Isabel of the Holy Sacrament of the Altar Castañeda y Montero, the bland parish priest who, at the age of ninety-four, assured people that he had seen the devil on three occasions, and that nevertheless he had only seen two dead birds, without attributing the least importance to them. He found the first one in the sacristy, one Tuesday after Mass, and thought it had been dragged in there by some neighborhood cat. He found the other one on Wednesday, in the veranda of the parish house, and he pushed it with the point of his boot into the street, thinking, Cats shouldn't exist.

But on Friday, when he arrived at the railroad station, he found a third dead bird on the bench he chose to sit down on. It was like a lightning stroke inside him when he grabbed the body by its little legs; he raised it to eye level, turned it over, examined it, and thought astonishedly, Gracious, this is the third one I've found this week.

From that moment on he began to notice what was happening in the town, but in a very inexact way, for Father Anthony Isabel, in part because of his age and in part also because he swore he had seen the devil on three occasions (something which seemed to the town just a bit out of place), was considered by his parishioners as a good man, peaceful and obliging, but with his head habitually in the clouds. He noticed that something was happening with the birds, but even then he didn't believe that it was so important as to deserve a sermon. He was the first one who experienced the smell. He smelled it Friday night, when he woke up alarmed, his light slumber interrupted by a nauseating stench, but he didn't know whether to attribute it to a nightmare or to a new and original trick of the devil's to disturb his sleep. He sniffed all around him, and turned over in bed, thinking that that experience would serve him for a sermon. It could be, he thought, a dramatic sermon on the ability of Satan to infiltrate the human heart through any of the five senses.

When he strolled around the porch the next day before Mass, he heard someone speak for the first time about the dead birds. He was thinking about the sermon, Satan, and the sins which can be committed through the olfactory sense when he heard someone say that the bad nocturnal odor was due to the birds collected during the week; and in his head a confused hodgepodge of evangelical cautions, evil odors, and dead birds took shape. So that on Sunday he had to improvise a long paragraph on Charity which he himself did not understand very well, and he forgot forever about the relations between the devil and the five senses.

Nevertheless, in some very distant spot in his thinking, those experiences must have remained lurking That always happened to him, not only in the seminary, more than seventy years before, but in a very particular way after he passed ninety. At the seminary, one very bright afternoon when there was a heavy downpour with no thunder, he was reading a selection from Sophocles in the original. When the rain was over, he looked through the window at the tired field, the newly washed afternoon, and forgot entirely about Greek theater and the classics, which he did not distinguish but, rather, called in a general way, "the little ancients of old." One rainless afternoon, perhaps thirty or forty years later, he was crossing the cobblestone plaza of a town which he was visiting and, without intending to, recited the stanza from Sophocles which he had been reading in the seminary. That same week, he had a long conversation about "the little ancients of old" with the apostolic deputy, a talkative and impressionable old man, who was fond of certain complicated puzzles which he claimed to have invented and which became popular years later under the name of crosswords.

That interview permitted him to recover at one stroke all his old heartfelt love for the Greek classics. At Christmas of that year he received a letter. And if it were not for the fact that by that time he had acquired the solid prestige of being exaggeratedly imaginative, daring in his interpretations, and a little foolish in his sermons, on that occasion they would have made him a bishop.

But he had buried himself in the town long before the War of 1885, and at the time when the birds began dying in the bedrooms it had been a long while since they had asked for him to be replaced by a younger priest, especially when he claimed to have seen the devil. From that time on they began not paying attention to him, something which he didn't notice in a very clear way in spite of still being able to decipher the tiny characters of his breviary without glasses.

He had always been a man of regular habits. Small, insignificant, with pronounced and solid bones and calm gestures, and a soothing voice for conversation but too soothing for the pulpit. He used to stay in his bedroom until lunchtime daydreaming, carelessly stretched out in a canvas chair and wearing nothing but his long twill trousers with the bottoms tied at the ankles.

He didn't do anything except say Mass. Twice a week he sat in the confessional, but for many years no one confessed. He

simply thought that his parishioners were losing the faith because of modern customs, and that's why he would have
thought it a very opportune occurrence to have seen the devil
on three occasions, although he knew that people gave very
little credence to his words and although he was aware that he
was not very convincing when he spoke about those experiences. For himself it would have been a surprise to discover
that he was dead, not only during the last five years but also
in those extraordinary moments when he found the first two
birds. When he found the third, however, he came back to life
a little, so that in the last few days he was thinking with ap-
preciable frequency about the dead bird on the station bench.

He lived ten steps from the church in a small house without
screens, with a veranda toward the street and two rooms which
served as office and bedroom. He considered, perhaps in his
moments of less lucidity, that it is possible to achieve happiness on earth when it is not very hot, and this idea made him
a little confused. He liked to wander through metaphysical
obstacle courses. That was what he was doing when he used
to sit in the bedroom every morning, with the door ajar, his
eyes closed and his muscles tensed. However, he himself did
not realize that he had become so subtle in his thinking that
for at least three years in his meditative moments he was no
longer thinking about anything.

At twelve o'clock sharp a boy crossed the corridor with a
sectioned tray which contained the same things every day:
bone broth with a piece of yucca, white rice, meat prepared
without onion, fried banana or a corn muffin, and a few lentils
which Father Anthony Isabel of the Holy Sacrament of the
Altar had never tasted.

The boy put the tray next to the chair where the priest sat,
but the priest didn't open his eyes until he no longer heard
steps in the corridor. Therefore, in town they thought that the

Father took his siesta before lunch (a thing which seemed exceedingly nonsensical) when the truth was that he didn't even sleep normally at night.

Around that time his habits had become less complicated, almost primitive. He lunched without moving from his canvas chair, without taking the food from the tray, without using the dishes or the fork or the knife, but only the same spoon with which he drank his soup. Later he would get up, throw a little water on his head, put on his white soutane dotted with great square patches, and go to the railroad station precisely at the hour when the rest of the town was lying down for its siesta. He had been covering this route for several months, murmuring the prayer which he himself had made up the last time the devil had appeared to him.

One Saturday—nine days after the dead birds began to fall— Father Anthony Isabel of the Holy Sacrament of the Altar was going to the station when a dying bird fell at his feet, directly in front of Rebecca's house. A flash of intuition exploded in his head, and he realized that this bird, contrary to the others, might be saved. He took it in his hands and knocked at Rebecca's door at the moment when she was unhooking her bodice to take her siesta.

In her bedroom, the widow heard the knocking and instinctively turned her glance toward the screens. No bird had got into that bedroom for two days. But the screen was still torn. She had thought it a useless expense to have it repaired as long as the invasion of birds, which kept her nerves on edge, continued. Above the hum of the electric fan, she heard the knocking at the door and remembered with impatience that Argenida was taking a siesta in the bedroom at the end of the corridor. It didn't even occur to her to wonder who might be imposing on her at that hour. She hooked up her bodice again, pushed open the screen door, and walked the length of the corridor, stiff and straight, then crossed the living room crowded with furniture and decorative objects and, before opening the door, saw through the metal screen that there stood taciturn Father Anthony Isabel, with his eyes closed and a bird in his hands. Before she opened the door, he said, "If we give him a little water and then put him under a dish, I'm sure he'll get well." And when she opened the door, Rebecca thought she'd collapse from fear.

He didn't stay there for more than five minutes. Rebecca thought that it was she who had cut short the meeting. But in reality it had been the priest. If the widow had thought about it at that moment, she would have realized that the priest, in the thirty years he had been living in the town, had never stayed more than five minutes in her house. It seemed to him that amid the profusion of decorations in the living room the concupiscent spirit of the mistress of the house showed itself clearly, in spite of her being related, however distantly, but as everyone was aware, to the Bishop. Furthermore, there had been a legend (or a story) about Rebecca's family which surely, the Father thought, had not reached the episcopal palace, in spite of the fact that Colonel Aureliano Buendía, a cousin of the widow's whom she considered lacking in family affection, had once sworn that the Bishop had not come to the town in this century in order to avoid visiting his relation. In any case, be it history or legend, the truth was that Father Anthony Isabel of the Holy Sacrament of the Altar did not feel at ease in this house, whose only inhabitant had never shown any signs of piety and who confessed only once a year but always replied with evasive answers when he tried to pin her down about the puzzling death of her husband. If he was there now, waiting for her to bring him a glass of water to bathe a dying bird, it was the result of a chance occurrence which he was not responsible for.

While he waited for the widow to return, the priest, seated on a luxurious carved wooden rocker, felt the strange humidity of that house which had not become peaceful since the time when a pistol shot rang out, more than twenty years before, and José Arcadio Buendía, cousin of the colonel and of his own wife, fell face down amidst the clatter of buckles and spurs on the still-warm leggings which he had just taken off.

When Rebecca burst into the living room again, she saw Father Anthony Isabel seated in the rocker with an air of vagueness which terrified her.

"The life of an animal," said the Father, "is as dear to Our Lord as that of a man."

As he said it, he did not remember José Arcadio Buendía. Nor did the widow recall him. But she was used to not giving any credence to the Father's words ever since he had spoken from the pulpit about the three times the devil had appeared to him. Without paying attention to him she took the bird in her hands, dipped him in the glass of water, and shook him afterward. The Father observed that there was impiety and carelessness in her way of acting, an absolute lack of consideration for the animal's life.

"You don't like birds," he said softly but affirmatively.

The widow raised her eyelids in a gesture of impatience and hostility. "Although I liked them once," she said, "I detest them now that they've taken to dying inside of our houses."

"Many have died," he said implacably. One might have thought that there was a great deal of cleverness in the even tone of his voice.

"All of them," said the widow. And she added, as she squeezed the animal with repugnance and placed him under the dish, "And even that wouldn't bother me if they hadn't torn my screens."

And it seemed to him that he had never known such hardness of heart. A moment later, holding the tiny and defenseless body in his own hand, the priest realized that it had ceased breathing. Then he forgot everything—the humidity of the house, the concupiscence, the unbearable smell of gunpowder on José Arcadio Buendía's body—and he realized the prodigious truth which had surrounded him since the beginning of the week. Right there, while the widow watched him leave the house with a menacing gesture and the dead bird in his hands, he witnessed the marvelous revelation that a rain of dead birds was falling over the town, and that he, the minister of God, the chosen one, who had known happiness when it had not been hot, had forgotten entirely about the Apocalypse.

That day he went to the station, as always, but he was not fully aware of his actions. He knew vaguely that something was happening in the world, but he felt muddled, dumb, unequal to the moment. Seated on the bench in the station, he tried to remember if there was a rain of dead birds in the Apocalypse, but he had forgotten it entirely. Suddenly he thought that his delay at Rebecca's house had made him miss the train, and he stretched his head up over the dusty and broken glass and saw on the clock in the ticket office that it was still twelve minutes to one. When he returned to the bench, he felt as if he were suffocating. At that moment he remembered it was Saturday. He moved his woven palm fan for a while, lost in his dark interior fog. Then he fretted over the buttons on his soutane and the buttons on his boots and over his long, snug, clerical trousers, and he noticed with alarm that he had never in his life been so hot.

Without moving from the bench he unbuttoned the collar of his soutane, took his handkerchief out of his sleeve, and wiped his flushed face, thinking, in a moment of illuminated pathos, that perhaps he was witnessing the unfolding of an earthquake. He had read that somewhere. Nevertheless the sky was clear: a transparent blue sky from which all the birds had mysteriously disappeared. He noticed the color and the transparency, but for a moment forgot about the dead birds. Now he was thinking about something else, about the possibility that a storm would break. Nevertheless the sky was diaphanous and tranquil, as if it were the sky over some other town, distant and different, where he had never felt the heat, and as if they were other eyes, not his own, which were looking at it. Then he looked toward the north, above the roofs of palms and rusted zinc, and saw the slow, silent, rhythmic blot of the buzzards over the dump.

For some mysterious reason, he relived at that moment the emotions he felt one Sunday in the seminary, shortly before taking his minor orders. The rector had given him permission to make use of his private library and he often stayed for hours and hours (especially on Sundays) absorbed in the reading of some yellowed books smelling of old wood, with annotations in Latin in the tiny, angular scrawl of the rector. One Sunday, after he had been reading for the whole day, the rector entered the room and rushed, shocked, to pick up a card which evidently had fallen from the pages of the book he was reading. He observed his superior's confusion with discreet indifference, but he managed to read the card. There was only one sentence, written in purple ink in a clean, straightforward hand: "Madame Ivette est morte cette nuit." More than half a century later, seeing a blot of buzzards over a forgotten town, he remembered the somber expression of the rector seated in front of him, purple against the dusk, his breathing imperceptibly quickened.

Shaken by that association, he did not then feel the heat, but rather exactly the reverse, the sting of ice in his groin and in the soles of his feet. He was terrified without knowing what the precise cause of that terror was, tangled in a net of confused ideas, among which it was impossible to distinguish a nauseating sensation, from Satan's hoof stuck in the mud, from a flock of dead birds falling on the world, while he, Anthony Isabel of the Holy Sacrament of the Altar, remained indifferent to that event. Then he straightened up, raised an awed hand, as if to begin a greeting which was lost in the void, and cried out in horror, "The Wandering Jew!"

At that moment the train whistled. For the first time in many years he did not hear it. He saw it pull into the station, surrounded by a dense cloud of smoke, and heard the rain of cinders against the sheets of rusted zinc. But that was like a distant and undecipherable dream from which he did not awaken completely until that afternoon, a little after four, when he put the finishing touches on the imposing sermon he would deliver on Sunday. Eight hours later, he was called to administer extreme unction to a woman.

With the result that the Father did not find out who arrived that afternoon on the train. For a long time he had watched the four cars go by, ramshackle and colorless, and he could not recall anyone's getting off to stay, at least in recent years. Before it was different, when he could spend a whole afternoon watching a train loaded with bananas go by; a hundred and forty cars loaded with fruit, passing endlessly until, well on toward nightfall, the last car passed with a man dangling a green lantern. Then he saw the town on the other side of the track—the lights were on now—and it seemed to him that, by merely watching the train pass, it had taken him to another town. Perhaps from that came his habit of being present at the station every day, even after they shot the workers to death and the banana plantations were finished, and with them the hundred-and-forty-car trains, and there was left only that yellow, dusty train which neither brought anyone nor took anyone away.

But that Saturday someone did come. When Father Anthony Isabel of the Holy Sacrament of the Altar left the station, a quiet boy with nothing particular about him except his hunger saw the priest from the window of the last car at the precise moment that he remembered he had not eaten since the previous day. He thought, If there's a priest, there

must be a hotel. And he got off the train and crossed the
street, which was blistered by the metallic August sun, and
entered the cool shade of a house located opposite the station
whence issued the sound of a worn gramophone record. His
sense of smell, sharpened by his two-day-old hunger, told him
that was the hotel. And he went in without seeing the sign
"HOTEL MACONDO," a sign which he was never to read in his
life.

The proprietress was more than five months pregnant. She
was the color of mustard, and looked exactly as her mother
had when her mother was pregnant with her. He ordered,
"Lunch, as quick as you can," and she, not trying to hurry,
served him a bowl of soup with a bare bone and some chopped
green banana in it. At that moment the train whistled. Absorbed in the warm and healthful vapor of the soup, he calculated the distance which lay between him and the station,
and immediately felt himself invaded by that confused sensation of panic which missing a train produces.

He tried to run. He reached the door, anguished, but he
hadn't even taken one step across the threshold when he
realized that he didn't have time to make the train. When he
returned to the table, he had forgotten his hunger; he saw a
girl next to the gramophone who looked at him pitifully, with
the horrible expression of a dog wagging his tail. Then, for
the first time that whole day, he took off his hat, which his
mother had given him two months before, and lodged it between his knees while he finished eating. When he got up
from the table, he didn't seem bothered by missing the train,
or by the prospect of spending a weekend in a town whose
name he would not take the trouble to find out. He sat down
in a corner of the room, the bones of his back supported by a
hard, straight chair, and stayed there for a long time, not listening to the records until the girl who was picking them out said:

"It's cooler on the veranda."

He felt ill. It took an effort to start conversation with strangers. He was afraid to look people in the face, and when he had no recourse but to speak, the words came out different from the way he thought them. "Yes," he replied. And he felt a slight shiver. He tried to rock, forgetting that he was not in a rocker.

"The people who come here pull a chair to the veranda since it's cooler," the girl said. And, listening to her, he realized how anxiously she wanted to talk. He risked a look at her just as she was winding up the gramophone. She seemed to have been sitting there for months, years perhaps, and she showed not the slightest interest in moving from that spot. She was winding up the gramophone but her life was concentrated on him. She was smiling.

"Thank you," he said, trying to get up, to put some ease and spontaneity into his movements. The girl didn't stop looking at him. She said, "They also leave their hats on the hook."

This time he felt a burning in his ears. He shivered, thinking about her way of suggesting things. He felt uncomfortably shut in, and again felt his panic over the missed train. But at that moment the proprietress entered the room.

"What are you doing?" she asked.

"He's pulling a chair onto the veranda, as they all do," the girl said.

He thought he perceived a mocking tone in her words.

"Don't bother," said the proprietress. "I'll bring you a stool."

The girl laughed and he left disconcerted. It was hot. An unbroken, dry heat, and he was sweating. The proprietress dragged a wooden stool with a leather seat to the veranda. He was about to follow her when the girl spoke again.

"The bad part about it is that the birds will frighten him," she said.

He managed to see the harsh look when the proprietress

turned her eyes on the girl. It was a swift but intense look. "What you should do is be quiet," she said, and turned smiling to him. Then he felt less alone and had the urge to speak.

"What was that she said?" he asked.

"That at this hour of the day dead birds fall onto the veranda," the girl said.

"Those are just some notions of hers," said the proprietress. She bent over to straighten a bouquet of artificial flowers on the little table in the middle of the room. There was a nervous twitch in her fingers.

"Notions of mine, no," the girl said. "You yourself swept two of them up the day before yesterday."

The proprietress looked exasperatedly at her. The girl had a pitiful expression, and an obvious desire to explain everything until not the slightest trace of doubt remained.

"What is happening, sir, is that the day before yesterday some boys left two dead birds in the hall to annoy her, and then they told her that dead birds were falling from the sky. She swallows everything people tell her."

He smiled. The explanation seemed very funny to him; he rubbed his hands and turned to look at the girl, who was observing him in anguish. The gramophone had stopped playing. The proprietress withdrew to the other room, and when he went toward the hall the girl insisted in a low voice:

"I saw them fall. Believe me. Everyone has seen them."

And he thought he understood then her attachment to the gramophone, and the proprietress's exasperation. "Yes," he said sympathetically. And then, moving toward the hall: "I've seen them, too."

It was less hot outside, in the shade of the almond trees. He leaned the stool against the doorframe, threw his head back, and thought of his mother: his mother, exhausted, in her rocker, shooing the chickens with a long broomstick, while she realized for the first time that he was not in the house.

The week before, he could have thought that his life was a smooth straight string, stretching from the rainy dawn during the last civil war when he came into the world between the four mud-and-rush walls of a rural schoolhouse to that June morning on his twenty-second birthday when his mother approached his hammock and gave him a hat with a card: "To my dear son, on his day." At times he shook off the rustiness of his inactivity and felt nostalgic for school, for the blackboard and the map of a country overpopulated by the excrement of the flies, and for the long line of cups hanging on the wall under the names of the children. It wasn't hot there. It was a green, tranquil town, where chickens with ashen long legs entered the schoolroom in order to lay their eggs under the washstand. His mother then was a sad and uncommunicative woman. She would sit at dusk to take the air which had just filtered through the coffee plantations, and say, "Manaure is the most beautiful town in the world." And then, turning toward him, seeing him grow up silently in the hammock: "When you are grown up you'll understand." But he didn't understand anything. He didn't understand at fifteen, already too tall for his age and bursting with that insolent and reckless health which idleness brings. Until his twentieth birthday his life was not essentially different from a few changes of position in his hammock. But around that time his mother, obliged by her rheumatism, left the school she had served for eighteen years, with the result that they went to live in a two-room house with a huge patio, where they raised chickens with ashen legs like those which used to cross the schoolroom.

Caring for the chickens was his first contact with reality. And it had been the only one until the month of July, when his mother thought about her retirement and deemed her son wise enough to undertake to petition for it. He collaborated in an effective way in the preparation of the documents, and even had the necessary tact to convince the parish priest to change his mother's baptismal certificate by six months, since she still wasn't old enough to retire. On Thursday he received the final instructions, scrupulously detailing his mother's teaching experience, and he began the trip to the city with twelve pesos, a change of clothing, the file of documents, and an entirely rudimentary idea of the word "retirement," which he interpreted crudely as a certain sum of money which the government ought to give him so he could set himself up in pig breeding.

Dozing on the hotel veranda, dulled by the sweltering heat, he had not stopped to think about the gravity of his situation. He supposed that the mishap would be resolved the following day, when the train returned, so that now his only worry was to wait until Sunday to resume his trip and forget forever about this town where it was unbearably hot. A little before four, he fell into an uncomfortable and sluggish sleep, thinking while he slept that it was a shame not to have brought his hammock. Then it was that he realized everything, that he had forgotten his bundle of clothes and the documents for the retirement on the train. He woke up with a start, terrified, thinking of his mother, and hemmed in again by panic.

When he dragged his seat back to the dining room, the lights of the town had been lit. He had never seen electric lights, so he was very impressed when he saw the poor spotted bulbs of the hotel. Then he remembered that his mother had spoken to him about them, and he continued dragging the seat toward the dining room, trying to dodge the horseflies which were bumping against the mirrors like bullets. He ate without appetite, confused by the clear evidence of his situation, by the intense heat, by the bitterness of that loneliness which he was suffering for the first time in his life. After nine o'clock he was led to the back of the house to a wooden room papered with newspapers and magazines. At midnight he had sunk into a miasmic and feverish sleep while, five blocks away, Father Anthony Isabel of the Holy Sacrament of the Altar, lying face down on his cot, was thinking that the evening's experiences reinforced the sermon which he had prepared for seven in the morning. A little before twelve he had crossed the town to administer extreme unction to a woman, and he felt excited and nervous, with the result that he put the sacramental objects next to his cot and lay down to go over his sermon. He stayed that way for several hours, lying face down on the cot until he heard the distant call of a plover at dawn. Then he tried to get up, sat up painfully, stepped on the little bell, and fell headlong on the cold, hard floor of his room.

He had hardly regained consciousness when he felt the trembling sensation which rose up his side. At that instant he was aware of his entire weight: the weight of his body, his sins, and his age all together. He felt against his cheek the solidity of the stone floor which so often when he was preparing his sermons had helped him form a precise idea of the road which leads to Hell. "Lord," he murmured, afraid; and he thought, I shall certainly never be able to get up again.

He did not know how long he lay prostrate on the floor, not thinking about anything, without even remembering to pray for a good death. It was as if, in reality, he had been dead for a minute. But when he regained consciousness, he no longer felt pain or fear. He saw the bright ray beneath the door; he heard, far off and sad, the raucous noise of the roosters, and he realized that he was alive and that he remembered the words of his sermon perfectly.

When he drew back the bar of the door, dawn was breaking. He had ceased feeling pain, and it even seemed that the blow had unburdened him of his old age. All the goodness, the misconduct, and the sufferings of the town penetrated his heart when he swallowed the first mouthful of that air which was a blue dampness full of roosters. Then he looked around himself, as if to reconcile himself to the solitude, and saw, in the peaceful shade of the dawn, one, two, three dead birds on the veranda.

For nine minutes he contemplated the three bodies, thinking, in accord with his prepared sermon, that the birds' collective death needed some expiation. Then he walked to the other end of the corridor, picked up the three dead birds and returned to the pitcher, and one after the other threw the birds into the green, still water without knowing exactly the purpose of that action. Three and three are half a dozen, in one week, he thought, and a miraculous flash of lucidity told him that he had begun to experience the greatest day of his life.

At seven the heat began. In the hotel, the only guest was waiting for his breakfast. The gramophone girl had not yet got up. The proprietress approached, and at that moment it seemed as if the seven strokes of the clock's bell were sounding inside her swollen belly.

"So you missed the train," she said in a tone of belated commiseration. And then she brought the breakfast: coffee with milk, a fried egg, and slices of green banana.

He tried to eat, but he wasn't hungry. He was alarmed that the heat had come on. He was sweating buckets. He was suffocating. He had slept poorly, with his clothes on, and now he had a little fever. He felt the panic again, and remembered his mother just as the proprietress came to the table to pick up the dishes, radiant in her new dress with the large green flowers. The proprietress's dress reminded him that it was Sunday.

"Is there a Mass?" he asked.

"Yes, there is," the woman said. "But it's just as if there weren't, because almost nobody goes. The fact is they haven't wanted to send us a new priest."

"And what's wrong with this one?"

"He's about a hundred years old, and he's half crazy," the woman said; she stood motionless, pensive, with all the dishes in one hand. Then she said, "The other day, he swore from the pulpit that he had seen the devil, and since then no one goes to Mass."

So he went to the church, in part because of his desperation and in part out of curiosity to meet a person a hundred years old. He noticed that it was a dead town, with interminable, dusty streets and dark wooden houses with zinc roofs, which seemed uninhabited. That was the town on Sunday: streets without grass, houses with screens, and a deep, marvelous sky over a stifling heat. He thought that there was no sign there which would permit one to distinguish Sunday from any other day, and while he walked along the deserted street he remembered his mother: "All the streets in every town lead inevitably to the church or the cemetery." At that moment he came out into a small cobblestoned plaza with a whitewashed building that had a tower and a wooden weathercock on the top, and a clock which had stopped at ten after four.

Without hurrying he crossed the plaza, climbed the three steps of the atrium, and immediately smelled the odor of aged human sweat mixed with the odor of incense, and he went into the warm shade of the almost empty church.

Father Anthony Isabel of the Holy Sacrament of the Altar had just risen to the pulpit. He was about to begin the sermon when he saw a boy enter with his hat on. He saw him examining the almost empty temple with his large, serene, and clear eyes. He saw him sit down in the last pew, his head to one side and his hands on his knees. He noticed that he was a stranger to the town. He had been in town for thirty years, and he could have recognized any of its inhabitants just by his smell. Therefore, he knew that the boy who had just arrived was a stranger. In one intense, brief look, he observed that he was a quiet soul, and a little sad, and that his clothes were dirty and wrinkled. It's as if he had spent a long time sleeping in them, he thought with a feeling that was a combination of repugnance and pity. But then, seeing him in the pew, he felt his heart overflowing with gratitude, and he got ready to deliver what was for him the greatest sermon of his life. Lord, he thought in the meantime, please let him remember his hat so I don't have to throw him out of the temple. And he began his sermon.

At the beginning he spoke without realizing what he was saying. He wasn't even listening to himself. He hardly heard the clear and fluent melody which flowed from a spring dormant in his soul ever since the beginning of the world. He had the confused certainty that his words were flowing forth precisely, opportunely, exactly, in the expected order and place. He felt a warm vapor pressing his innards. But he also knew that his spirit was free of vanity, and that the feeling of pleasure which paralyzed his senses was not pride or defiance or vanity but, rather, the pure rejoicing of his spirit in Our Lord.

In her bedroom, Rebecca felt faint, knowing that within a few moments the heat would become impossible. If she had not felt rooted to the town by a dark fear of novelty, she would have put her odds and ends in a trunk with mothballs and would have gone off into the world, as her great-grandfather did, so she had been told. But she knew inside that she was destined to die in the town, amid those endless corridors and the nine bedrooms, whose screens she thought she would have replaced by translucent glass when the heat stopped. So she would stay there, she decided (and that was a decision she always took when she arranged her clothes in the closet), and she also decided to write "My Eminent Cousin" to send them a young priest, so she could attend church again with her hat with the tiny velvet flowers, and hear a coherent Mass and sensible and edifying sermons again. Tomorrow is Monday, she thought, beginning to think once and for all about the salutation of the letter to the Bishop (a salutation which Colonel Buendía had called frivolous and disrespectful), when Argenida suddenly opened the screened door and shouted:

"Señora, people are saying that the Father has gone crazy in the pulpit!"

The widow turned a not characteristically withered and bitter face toward the door. "He's been crazy for at least five years," she said. And she kept on arranging her clothing, saying:

"He must have seen the devil again."

"It's not the devil this time," said Argenida.

"Then who?" Rebecca asked, prim and indifferent.

"Now he says that he saw the Wandering Jew."

The widow felt her skin crawl. A multitude of confused ideas, among which she could not distinguish her torn screens, the heat, the dead birds, and the plague, passed through her head as she heard those words which she hadn't remembered since the afternoons of her distant girlhood: "The Wandering Jew." And then she began to move, enraged, icily, toward where Argenida was watching her with her mouth open.

"It's true," Rebecca said in a voice which rose from the depths of her being. "Now I understand why the birds are dying off."

Impelled by terror, she covered herself with a black embroidered shawl and, in a flash, crossed the long corridor and the living room stuffed with decorative objects, and the street door, and the two blocks to the church, where Father Anthony Isabel of the Holy Sacrament of the Altar, transfigured, was saying, "I swear to you that I saw him. I swear to you that he crossed my path this morning when I was coming back from administering the holy unction to the wife of Jonas the carpenter. I swear to you that his face was blackened with the malediction of the Lord, and that he left a track of burning embers in his wake."

His sermon broke off, floating in the air. He realized that he couldn't restrain the trembling of his hands, that his whole body was shaking, and that a thread of icy sweat was slowly descending his spinal column. He felt ill, feeling the trembling, and the thirst, and a violent wrenching in his gut, and a noise which resounded like the bass note of an organ in his belly. Then he realized the truth.

He saw that there were people in the church, and that Rebecca, pathetic, showy, her arms open, and her bitter, cold face turned toward the heavens, was advancing up the central nave. Confusedly he understood what was happening, and he even had enough lucidity to understand that it would have been vanity to believe that he was witnessing a miracle. Humbly he rested his trembling hands on the wooden edge of the pulpit and resumed his speech.

"Then he walked toward me," he said. And this time he heard his own voice, convincing, impassioned. "He walked toward me and he had emerald eyes, and shaggy hair, and the smell of a billy goat. And I raised my hand to reproach him in the name of Our Lord, and I said to him: 'Halt, Sunday has never been a good day for sacrificing a lamb.' "

When he finished, the heat had set in. That intense, solid, burning heat of that unforgettable August. But Father Anthony Isabel was no longer aware of the heat. He knew that there, at his back, the town was again humbled, speechless with his sermon, but he wasn't even pleased by that. He wasn't even pleased with the immediate prospect that the wine would relieve his ravaged throat. He felt uncomfortable and out of place. He felt distracted and he could not concentrate on the supreme moment of the sacrifice. The same thing had been happening to him for some time, but now it was a different distraction, because his thoughts were filled by a definite uneasiness. Then, for the first time in his life, he knew pride. And just as he had imagined and defined it in his sermons, he felt that pride was an urge the same as thirst. He closed the tabernacle energetically and said:

"Pythagoras."

The acolyte, a child with a shaven and shiny head, godson of Father Anthony Isabel, who had named him, approached the altar.

"Take up the offering," said the priest.

The child blinked, turned completely around, and then said in an almost inaudible voice, "I don't know where the plate is."

It was true. It had been months since an offering had been collected.

"Then go find a big bag in the sacristy and collect as much as you can," said the Father.

"And what shall I say?" said the boy.

The Father thoughtfully contemplated his shaven blue skull, with its prominent sutures. Now it was he who blinked:

"Say that it is to expel the Wandering Jew," he said, and he felt as he said it that he was supporting a great weight in his heart. For a moment he heard nothing but the guttering of the candles in the silent temple and his own excited and labored breathing. Then, putting his hand on the acolyte's shoulder, while the acolyte looked at him with his round eyes aghast, he said:

"Then take the money and give it to the boy who was alone at the beginning, and you tell him that it's from the priest, and that he should buy a new hat."

ARTIFICIAL ROSES

FEELING HER WAY in the gloom of dawn, Mina put on the sleeveless dress which the night before she had hung next to the bed, and rummaged in the trunk for the detachable sleeves. Then she looked for them on the nails on the walls, and behind the doors, trying not to make noise so as not to wake her blind grandmother, who was sleeping in the same room. But when she got used to the darkness, she noticed that the grandmother had got up, and she went into the kitchen to ask her for the sleeves.

"They're in the bathroom," the blind woman said. "I washed them yesterday afternoon."

There they were, hanging from a wire with two wooden clothespins. They were still wet. Mina went back into the kitchen and stretched the sleeves out on the stones of the fireplace. In front of her, the blind woman was stirring the coffee, her dead pupils fixed on the stone border of the veranda, where there was a row of flowerpots with medicinal herbs.

"Don't take my things again," said Mina. "These days, you can't count on the sun."

The blind woman moved her face toward the voice.

"I had forgotten that it was the first Friday," she said.

After testing with a deep breath to see if the coffee was ready, she took the pot off the fire.

"Put a piece of paper underneath, because these stones are dirty," she said.

Mina ran her index finger along the fireplace stones. They were dirty, but with a crust of hardened soot which would not dirty the sleeves if they were not rubbed against the stones.

"If they get dirty you're responsible," she said.

146

The blind woman had poured herself a cup of coffee. "You're angry," she said, pulling a chair toward the veranda. "It's a sacrilege to take Communion when one is angry." She sat down to drink her coffee in front of the roses in the patio. When the third call for Mass rang, Mina took the sleeves off the fireplace and they were still wet. But she put them on. Father Angel would not give her Communion with a bare-shouldered dress on. She didn't wash her face. She took off the traces of rouge with a towel, picked up the prayer book and shawl in her room, and went into the street. A quarter of an hour later she was back.

"You'll get there after the reading of the gospel," the blind woman said, seated opposite the roses in the patio.

Mina went directly to the toilet. "I can't go to Mass," she said. "The sleeves are wet, and my whole dress is wrinkled." She felt a knowing look follow her.

"First Friday and you're not going to Mass," exclaimed the blind woman.

Back from the toilet, Mina poured herself a cup of coffee and sat down against the whitewashed doorway, next to the blind woman. But she couldn't drink the coffee.

"You're to blame," she murmured, with a dull rancor, feeling that she was drowning in tears.

"You're crying," the blind woman exclaimed.

She put the watering can next to the pots of oregano and went out into the patio, repeating, "You're crying." Mina put her cup on the ground before sitting up.

"I'm crying from anger," she said. And added, as she passed next to her grandmother, "You must go to confession because you made me miss the first-Friday Communion."

The blind woman remained motionless, waiting for Mina to close the bedroom door. Then she walked to the end of the veranda. She bent over haltingly until she found the untouched cup in one piece on the ground. While she poured the coffee into the earthen pot, she went on:

"God knows I have a clear conscience."

Mina's mother came out of the bedroom.

"Who are you talking to?" she asked.

"To no one," said the blind woman. "I've told you already that I'm going crazy."

Ensconced in her room, Mina unbuttoned her bodice and took out three little keys which she carried on a safety pin. With one of the keys she opened the lower drawer of the armoire and took out a miniature wooden trunk. She opened it with another key. Inside there was a packet of letters written on colored paper, held together by a rubber band. She hid them in her bodice, put the little trunk in its place, and locked the drawer. Then she went to the toilet and threw the letters in.

"I thought you were at church," her mother said when Mina came into the kitchen.

"She couldn't go," the blind woman interrupted. "I forgot that it was first Friday, and I washed the sleeves yesterday afternoon."

"They're still wet," murmured Mina.

"I've had to work hard these days," the blind woman said.

"I have to deliver a hundred and fifty dozen roses for Easter," Mina said.

The sun warmed up early. Before seven Mina set up her artificial-rose shop in the living room: a basket full of petals and wires, a box of crêpe paper, two pairs of scissors, a spool of thread, and a pot of glue. A moment later Trinidad arrived, with a pasteboard box under her arm, and asked her why she hadn't gone to Mass.

"I didn't have any sleeves," said Mina.

"Anyone could have lent some to you," said Trinidad.

She pulled over a chair and sat down next to the basket of petals.

"I was too late," Mina said.

She finished a rose. Then she pulled the basket closer to shirr the petals with the scissors. Trinidad put the pasteboard box on the floor and joined in the work.

Mina looked at the box.

"Did you buy shoes?" she asked.

"They're dead mice," said Trinidad.

Since Trinidad was an expert at shirring petals, Mina spent her time making stems of wire wound with green paper. They worked silently without noticing the sun advance in the living room, which was decorated with idyllic prints and family photographs. When she finished the stems, Mina turned toward Trinidad with a face that seemed to end in something immaterial. Trinidad shirred with admirable neatness, hardly moving the petal tip between her fingers, her legs close together. Mina observed her masculine shoes. Trinidad avoided the look without raising her head, barely drawing her feet backward, and stopped working.

"What's the matter?" she said.

Mina leaned toward her.

"He went away," she said.

Trinidad dropped the scissors in her lap.

"No."

"He went away," Mina repeated.

Trinidad looked at her without blinking. A vertical wrinkle divided her knit brows.

"And now?" she asked.

Mina replied in a steady voice.

"Now nothing."

Trinidad said goodbye before ten.

Freed from the weight of her intimacy, Mina stopped her a

moment to throw the dead mice into the toilet. The blind woman was pruning the rosebush.

"I'll bet you don't know what I have in this box," Mina said to her as she passed.

She shook the mice.

The blind woman began to pay attention. "Shake it again," she said. Mina repeated the movement, but the blind woman could not identify the objects after listening for a third time with her index finger pressed against the lobe of her ear.

"They are the mice which were caught in the church traps last night," said Mina.

When she came back, she passed next to the blind woman without speaking. But the blind woman followed her. When she got to the living room, Mina was alone next to the closed window, finishing the artificial roses.

"Mina," said the blind woman. "If you want to be happy, don't confess with strangers."

Mina looked at her without speaking. The blind woman sat down in the chair in front of her and tried to help with the work. But Mina stopped her.

"You're nervous," said the blind woman.

"Why didn't you go to Mass?" asked the blind woman.

"You know better than anyone."

"If it had been because of the sleeves, you wouldn't have bothered to leave the house," said the blind woman. "Someone was waiting for you on the way who caused you some disappointment."

Mina passed her hands before her grandmother's eyes, as if cleaning an invisible pane of glass.

"You're a witch," she said.

"You went to the toilet twice this morning," the blind woman said. "You never go more than once."

Mina kept making roses.

"Would you dare show me what you are hiding in the drawer of the armoire?" the blind woman asked.

Unhurriedly, Mina stuck the rose in the window frame, took the three little keys out of her bodice, and put them in the blind woman's hand. She herself closed her fingers.

"Go see with your own eyes," she said.

The blind woman examined the little keys with her finger-tips.

"My eyes cannot see down the toilet."

Mina raised her head and then felt a different sensation: she felt that the blind woman knew that she was looking at her.

"Throw yourself down the toilet if what I do is so interesting to you," she said.

The blind woman ignored the interruption.

"You always stay up writing in bed until early morning," she said.

"You yourself turn out the light," Mina said.

"And immediately you turn on the flashlight," the blind woman said. "I can tell that you're writing by your breathing."

Mina made an effort to stay calm. "Fine," she said without raising her head. "And supposing that's the way it is. What's so special about it?"

"Nothing," replied the blind woman. "Only that it made you miss first-Friday Communion."

With both hands Mina picked up the spool of thread, the scissors, and a fistful of unfinished stems and roses. She put it all in the basket and faced the blind woman. "Would you like me to tell you what I went to do in the toilet, then?" she asked. They both were in suspense until Mina replied to her own question:

"I went to take a shit."

The blind woman threw the three little keys into the basket. "It would be a good excuse," she murmured, going into the kitchen. "You would have convinced me if it weren't the first time in your life I've ever heard you swear." Mina's mother was coming along the corridor in the opposite direction, her arms full of bouquets of thorned flowers.

"What's going on?" she asked.

"I'm crazy," said the blind woman. "But apparently you haven't thought of sending me to the madhouse so long as I don't start throwing stones."

BIG MAMA'S FUNERAL

THIS IS, for all the world's unbelievers, the true account of Big Mama, absolute sovereign of the Kingdom of Macondo, who lived for ninety-two years, and died in the odor of sanctity one Tuesday last September, and whose funeral was attended by the Pope.

Now that the nation, which was shaken to its vitals, has recovered its balance; now that the bagpipers of San Jacinto, the smugglers of Guajira, the rice planters of Sinú, the prostitutes of Caucamayal, the wizards of Sierpe, and the banana workers of Aracataca have folded up their tents to recover from the exhausting vigil and have regained their serenity, and the President of the Republic and his Ministers and all those who represented the public and supernatural powers on the most magnificent funeral occasion recorded in the annals of history have regained control of their estates; now that the Holy Pontiff has risen up to Heaven in body and soul; and now that it is impossible to walk around in Macondo because of the empty bottles, the cigarette butts, the gnawed bones, the cans and rags and excrement that the crowd which came to the burial left behind; now is the time to lean a stool against the front door and relate from the beginning the details of this national commotion, before the historians have a chance to get at it.

Fourteen weeks ago, after endless nights of poultices, mustard plasters, and leeches, and weak with the delirium of her death agony, Big Mama ordered them to seat her in her old rattan rocker so she could express her last wishes. It was the only thing she needed to do before she died. That morning, with the intervention of Father Anthony Isabel, she had put the affairs of her soul in order, and now she needed only to put her worldy affairs in order with her nine nieces and nephews, her sole heirs, who were standing around her bed. The priest, talking to himself and on the verge of his hundredth birthday, stayed in the room. Ten men had been needed to take him up to Big Mama's bedroom, and it was decided that he should stay there so they should not have to take him down and then take him up again at the last minute.

Nicanor, the eldest nephew, gigantic and savage, dressed in khaki and spurred boots, with a .38-caliber long-barreled revolver holstered under his shirt, went to look for the notary. The enormous two-story mansion, fragrant from molasses and oregano, with its dark apartments crammed with chests and the odds and ends of four generations turned to dust, had become paralyzed since the week before, in expectation of that moment. In the long central hall, with hooks on the walls where in another time butchered pigs had been hung and deer were slaughtered on sleepy August Sundays, the peons were sleeping on farm equipment and bags of salt, awaiting the order to saddle the mules to spread the bad news to the four corners of the huge hacienda. The rest of the family was in the living room. The women were limp, exhausted by the inheritance proceedings and lack of sleep; they kept a strict mourning which was the culmination of countless accumulated mournings. Big Mama's matriarchal rigidity had surrounded her fortune and her name with a sacramental fence, within which uncles married the daughters of their nieces, and the cousins married their aunts, and brothers their sisters-in-law, until an intricate mesh of consanguinity was formed, which turned procreation into a vicious circle. Only Magdalena, the youngest of the nieces, managed to escape it. Terrified by hallucinations, she made Father Anthony Isabel exorcise her, shaved her head, and renounced the glories and vanities of the world in the novitiate of the Mission District.

On the margin of the official family, and in exercise of the *jus primae noctis*, the males had fertilized ranches, byways, and settlements with an entire bastard line, which circulated among the servants without surnames, as godchildren, employees, favorites, and protégés of Big Mama.

The imminence of her death stirred the exhausting expectation. The dying woman's voice, accustomed to homage and obedience, was no louder than a bass organ pipe in the closed room, but it echoed in the most far-flung corners of the hacienda. No one was indifferent to this death. During this century, Big Mama had been Macondo's center of gravity, as had her brothers, her parents, and the parents of her parents in the past, in a dominance which covered two centuries. The town was founded on her surname. No one knew the origin, or the limits or the real value of her estate, but everyone was used to believing that Big Mama was the owner of the waters, running and still, of rain and drought, and of the district's roads, telegraph poles, leap years, and heat waves, and that she had furthermore a hereditary right over life and property. When she sat on her balcony in the cool afternoon air, with all the weight of her belly and authority squeezed into her old rattan rocker, she seemed, in truth, infinitely rich and powerful, the richest and most powerful matron in the world.

It had not occurred to anyone to think that Big Mama was mortal, except the members of her tribe, and Big Mama herself, prodded by the senile premonitions of Father Anthony Isabel. But she believed that she would live more than a hundred years, as did her maternal grandmother, who in the War of 1885 confronted a patrol of Colonel Aureliano Buendía's, barricaded in the kitchen of the hacienda. Only in April of this year did Big Mama realize that God would not grant her the privilege of personally liquidating, in an open skirmish, a horde of Federalist Masons.

During the first week of pain, the family doctor maintained her with mustard plasters and woolen stockings. He was hereditary doctor, a graduate of Montpellier, hostile by philo-sophical conviction to the progress of his science, whom Big Mama had accorded the lifetime privilege of preventing the es-tablishment in Macondo of any other doctors. At one time he covered the town on horseback, visiting the doleful, sick people at dusk, and Nature had accorded him the privilege of being the father of many another's children. But arthritis kept him stiff-jointed in bed, and he ended up attending to his patients without calling on them, by means of suppositions, messengers, and errands. Summoned by Big Mama, he crossed the plaza in his pajamas, leaning on two canes, and he installed himself in the sick woman's bedroom. Only when he realized that Big Mama was dying did he order a chest with porcelain jars labeled in Latin brought, and for three weeks he besmeared the dying woman inside and out with all sorts of academic salves, magnificent stimulants, and masterful suppositories. Then he applied bloated toads to the site of her pain, and leaches to her kidneys, until the early morning of that day when he had to face the dilemma of either having her bled by the barber or exorcised by Father Anthony Isabel.

Nicanor sent for the priest. His ten best men carried him from the parish house to Big Mama's bedroom, seated on a creaking willow rocker, under the mildewed canopy reserved for great occasions. The little bell of the Viaticum in the warm September dawn was the first notification to the inhabitants of Macondo. When the sun rose, the little plaza in front of Big Mama's house looked like a country fair.

It was like a memory of another era. Until she was seventy, Big Mama used to celebrate her birthday with the most pro-longed and tumultuous carnivals within memory. Demijohns of rum were placed at the townspeople's disposal, cattle were sacrificed in the public plaza, and a band installed on top of table played for three days without stopping. Under the sty almond trees, where, in the first week of the century,

Colonel Aureliano Buendía's troops had camped, stalls were set up which sold banana liquor, rolls, blood puddings, chopped fried meat, meat pies, sausage, yucca breads, crullers, buns, corn breads, puff pastes, *longanizas*, tripes, coconut nougats, rum toddies, along with all sorts of trifles, gewgaws, trinkets, and knicknacks, and cockfights and lottery tickets. In the midst of the confusion of the agitated mob, prints and scapularies with Big Mama's likeness were sold.

The festivities used to begin two days before and end on the day of her birthday, with the thunder of fireworks and a family dance at Big Mama's house. The carefully chosen guests and the legitimate members of the family, generously attended by the bastard line, danced to the beat of the old pianola which was equipped with the rolls most in style. Big Mama presided over the party from the rear of the hall in an easy chair with linen pillows, imparting discreet instructions with her right hand, adorned with rings on all her fingers. On that night the coming year's marriages were arranged, at times in complicity with the lovers, but almost always counseled by her own inspiration. To finish off the jubilation, Big Mama went out to the balcony, which was decorated with diadems and Japanese lanterns, and threw coins to the crowd.

That tradition had been interrupted, in part because of the successive mournings of the family and in part because of the political instability of the last few years. The new generations only heard stories of those splendid celebrations. They never managed to see Big Mama at High Mass, fanned by some functionary of the Civil Authority, enjoying the privilege of not kneeling, even at the moment of the elevation, so as not to ruin her Dutch-flounced skirt and her starched cambric petticoats. The old people remembered, like a hallucination out of their youth, the two hundred yards of matting which were laid down from the manorial house to the main altar the afternoon on which Maria del Rosario Castañeda y Montero attended her father's funeral and returned along the matted street endowed with a new and radiant dignity, turned into Big Mama at the age of twenty-two. That medieval vision belonged then not only to the family's past but also to the nation's past. Ever more indistinct and remote, hardly visible on her balcony, stifled by the geraniums on hot afternoons, Big Mama was melting into her own legend. Her authority was exercised through Nicanor. The tacit promise existed, formulated by tradition, that the day Big Mama sealed her will the heirs would declare three nights of public merrymaking. But at the same time it was known that she had decided not to express her last wishes until a few hours before dying, and no one thought seriously about the possibility that Big Mama was mortal. Only this morning, awakened by the tinkling of the Viaticum, did the inhabitants of Macondo become convinced not only that Big Mama was mortal but also that she was dying.

Her hour had come. Seeing her in her linen bed, bedaubed with aloes up to her ears, under the dust-laden canopy of Oriental crêpe, one could hardly make out any life in the thin respiration of her matriarchal breasts. Big Mama, who until she was fifty rejected the most passionate suitors, and who was well enough endowed by Nature to suckle her whole issue all by herself, was dying a virgin and childless. At the moment of extreme unction, Father Anthony Isabel had to ask for help in order to apply the oils to the palms of her hands, for since the beginning of her death throes Big Mama had had her fists closed. The attendance of the nieces was useless. In the struggle, for the first time in a week, the dying woman pressed against her chest the hand bejeweled with precious stones and fixed her colorless look on the nieces, saying, "Highway robbers." Then she saw Father Anthony Isabel in his liturgical habit and the acolyte with the sacramental implements, and with calm conviction she murmured, "I am dying." Then

she took off the ring with the great diamond and gave it to
Magdalena, the novice, to whom it belonged since she was the
youngest heir. That was the end of a tradition: Magdalena had
renounced her inheritance in favor of the Church.

At dawn Big Mama asked to be left alone with Nicanor to
impart her last instructions. For half an hour, in perfect com-
mand of her faculties, she asked about the conduct of her
affairs. She gave special instructions about the disposition of
her body, and finally concerned herself with the wake. "You
have to keep your eyes open," she said. "Keep everything of
value under lock and key, because many people come to wakes
only to steal." A moment later, alone with the priest, she made
an extravagant confession, sincere and detailed, and later on
took Communion in the presence of her nieces and nephews.
It was then that she asked them to seat her in her rattan rocker
so that she could express her last wishes.

Nicanor had prepared, on twenty-four folios written in a
very clear hand, a scrupulous account of her possessions.
Breathing calmly, with the doctor and Father Anthony Isabel
as witnesses, Big Mama dictated to the notary the list of her
property, the supreme and unique source of her grandeur and
authority. Reduced to its true proportions, the real estate was
limited to three districts, awarded by Royal Decree at the
founding of the Colony; with the passage of time, by dint of
intricate marriages of convenience, they had accumulated
under the control of Big Mama. In that unworked territory,
without definite borders, which comprised five townships and
in which not one single grain had ever been sown at the expense of the proprietors, three hundred and fifty-two families
lived as tenant farmers. Every year, on the eve of her name
day, Big Mama exercised the only act of control which prevented the lands from reverting to the state: the collection of
rent. Seated on the back porch of her house, she personally
received the payment for the right to live on her lands, as fo

more than a century her ancestors had received it from the ancestors of the tenants. When the three-day collection was over, the patio was crammed with pigs, turkeys, and chickens, and with the tithes and first fruits of the land which were deposited there as gifts. In reality, that was the only harvest the family ever collected from a territory which had been dead since its beginnings, and which was calculated on first examination at a hundred thousand hectares. But historical circumstances had brought it about that within those boundaries the six towns of Macondo district should grow and prosper, even the county seat, so that no person who lived in a house had any property rights other than those which pertained to the house itself, since the land belonged to Big Mama, and the rent was paid to her, just as the government had to pay her for the use the citizens made of the streets.

On the outskirts of the settlements, a number of animals, never counted and even less looked after, roamed, branded on the hindquarters with the shape of a padlock. This hereditary brand, which more out of disorder than out of quantity had become familiar in distant districts where the scattered cattle, dying of thirst, strayed in summer, was one of the most solid supports of the legend. For reasons which no one had bothered to explain, the extensive stables of the house had progressively emptied since the last civil war, and lately sugar-cane presses, milking parlors, and a rice mill had been installed in them.

Aside from the items enumerated, she mentioned in her will the existence of three containers of gold coins buried somewhere in the house during the War of Independence, which had not been found after periodic and laborious excavations. Along with the right to continue the exploitation of the rented land, and to receive the tithes and first fruits and all sorts of extraordinary donations, the heirs received a chart kept up from generation to generation, and perfected by each generation, which facilitated the finding of the buried treasure.

Big Mama needed three hours to enumerate her earthly possessions. In the stifling bedroom, the voice of the dying woman seemed to dignify in its place each thing named. When she affixed her trembling signature, and the witnesses affixed theirs below, a secret tremor shook the hearts of the crowds which were beginning to gather in front of the house, in the shade of the dusty almond trees of the plaza.

The only thing lacking then was the detailed listing of her immaterial possessions. Making a supreme effort—the same kind that her forebears made before they died to assure the dominance of their line—Big Mama raised herself up on her monumental buttocks, and in a domineering and sincere voice, lost in her memories, dictated to the notary this list of her invisible estate:

The wealth of the subsoil, the territorial waters, the colors of the flag, national sovereignty, the traditional parties, the rights of man, civil rights, the nation's leadership, the right of appeal, Congressional hearings, letters of recommendation, historical records, free elections, beauty queens, transcendental speeches, huge demonstrations, distinguished young ladies, proper gentlemen, punctilious military men, His Illustrious Eminence, the Supreme Court, goods whose importation was forbidden, liberal ladies, the meat problem, the purity of the language, setting a good example, the free but responsible press, the Athens of South America, public opinion, the lessons of democracy, Christian morality, the shortage of foreign exchange, the right of asylum, the Communist menace, the ship of state, the high cost of living, republican traditions, the underprivileged classes, statements of political support.

She didn't manage to finish. The laborious enumeration cut off her last breath. Drowning in the pandemonium of abstract formulas which for two centuries had constituted the moral justification of the family's power, Big Mama emitted a loud belch and expired.

That afternoon the inhabitants of the distant and somber capital saw the picture of a twenty-year-old woman on the first page of the extra editions, and thought that it was a new beauty queen. Big Mama lived again the momentary youth of her photograph, enlarged to four columns and with needed retouching, her abundant hair caught up atop her skull with an ivory comb and a diadem on her lace collar. That image, captured by a street photographer who passed through Macondo at the beginning of the century, and kept in the newspaper's morgue for many years in the section of unidentified persons, was destined to endure in the memory of future generations. In the dilapidated buses, in the elevators at the Ministries, and in the dismal tearooms hung with pale decorations, people whispered with veneration and respect about the dead personage in her sultry, malarial region, whose name was unknown in the rest of the country a few hours before—before it had been sanctified by the printed word. A fine drizzle covered the passers-by with misgiving and mist. All the church bells tolled for the dead. The President of the Republic, taken by surprise by the news when on his way to the commencement exercises for the new cadets, suggested to the War Minister, in a note in his own hand on the back of the telegram, that he conclude his speech with a minute of silent homage to Big Mama.

The social order had been brushed by death. The President of the Republic himself, who was affected by urban feelings as if they reached him through a purifying filter, managed to perceive from his car in a momentary but to a certain extent brutal vision the silent consternation of the city. Only a few low cafés remained open; the Metropolitan Cathedral was readied for nine days of funeral rites. At the National Capitol, where the beggars wrapped in newspapers slept in the shelter of the Doric columns and the silent statues of dead Presidents, the lights of Congress were lit. When the President entered is office, moved by the vision of the capital in mourning, his

Ministers were waiting for him dressed in funereal garb, standing, paler and more solemn than usual.

The events of that night and the following ones would later be identified as a historic lesson. Not only because of the Christian spirit which inspired the most lofty personages of public power, but also because of the abnegation with which dissimilar interests and conflicting judgments were conciliated in the common goal of burying the illustrious body. For many years Big Mama had guaranteed the social peace and political harmony of her empire, by virtue of the three trunks full of forged electoral certificates which formed part of her secret estate. The men in her service, her protégés and tenants, elder and younger, exercised not only their own rights of suffrage but also those of electors dead for a century. She exercised the priority of traditional power over transitory authority, the predominance of class over the common people, the transcendence of divine wisdom over human improvisation. In times of peace, her dominant will approved and disapproved canonries, benefices, and sinecures, and watched over the welfare of her associates, even if she had to resort to clandestine maneuvers or election fraud in order to obtain it. In troubled times, Big Mama contributed secretly for weapons for her partisans, but came to the aid of her victims in public. That patriotic zeal guaranteed the highest honors for her.

The President of the Republic had not needed to consult with his advisers in order to weigh the gravity of his responsibility. Between the Palace reception hall and the little paved patio which had served the viceroys as a cochère, there was an interior garden of dark cypresses where a Portuguese monk had hanged himself out of love in the last days of the Colony. Despite his noisy coterie of bemedaled officials, the President could not suppress a slight tremor of uncertainty when he passed that spot after dusk. But that night his trembling had the strength of a premonition. Then the full awareness of his historical destiny dawned on him, and he decreed nine days of national mourning, and posthumous honors for Big Mama at the rank befitting a heroine who had died for the fatherland on the field of battle. As he expressed it in the dramatic address which he delivered that morning to his compatriots over the national radio and television network, the Nation's Leader trusted that the funeral rites for Big Mama would set a new example for the world.

Such a noble aim was to collide nevertheless with certain grave inconveniences. The judicial structure of the country, built by remote ancestors of Big Mama, was not prepared for events such as those which began to occur. Wise Doctors of Law, certified alchemists of the statutes, plunged into hermeneutics and syllogisms in search of the formula which would permit the President of the Republic to attend the funeral. The upper strata of politics, the clergy, the financiers lived through entire days of alarm. In the vast semicircle of Congress, rarefied by a century of abstract legislation, amid oil paintings of National Heroes and busts of Greek thinkers, the vocation of Big Mama reached unheard-of proportions, while her body filled with bubbles in the harsh Macondo September. For the first time, people spoke of her and conceived of her without her rattan rocker, her afternoon stupors, and her mustard plasters, and they saw her ageless and pure, distilled by legend.

Interminable hours were filled with words, words, words, which resounded throughout the Republic, made prestigious by the spokesmen of the printed word. Until, endowed with a sense of reality in that assembly of aseptic lawgivers, the historic blahblahblah was interrupted by the reminder that Big Mama's corpse awaited their decision at 104° in the shade. No one batted an eye in the face of that eruption of common sense in the pure atmosphere of the written law. Orders were issued to embalm the cadaver, while formulas were adduced, viewpoints were reconciled, or constitutional amendments were made to permit the President to attend the burial.

So much had been said that the discussions crossed the borders, traversed the ocean, and blew like an omen through the pontifical apartments at Castel Gandolfo. Recovered from the drowsiness of the torpid days of August, the Supreme Pontiff was at the window watching the lake where the divers were searching for the head of a decapitated young girl. For the last few weeks, the evening newspapers had been concerned with nothing else, and the Supreme Pontiff could not be indifferent to an enigma located such a short distance from his summer residence. But that evening, in an unforeseen substitution, the newspapers changed the photographs of the possible victims for that of one single twenty-year-old woman, marked off with black margins. "Big Mama," exclaimed the Supreme Pontiff, recognizing instantly the hazy daguerreotype which many years before had been offered to him on the occasion of his ascent to the Throne of Saint Peter. "Big Mama," exclaimed in chorus the members of the College of Cardinals in their private apartments, and for the third time in twenty centuries there was an hour of confusion, chagrin, and bustle in the limitless empire of Christendom, until the Supreme Pontiff was installed in his long black limousine en route to Big Mama's fantastic and far-off funeral.

The shining peach orchards were left behind, the Via Appia Antica with warm movie stars tanning on terraces without as yet having heard any news of the commotion, and then the somber promontory of Castel Sant' Angelo on the edge of the Tiber. At dusk the resonant pealing of St. Peter's Basilica mingled with the cracked tinklings of Macondo. Inside his stifling tent across the tangled reeds and the silent bogs which marked the boundary between the Roman Empire and the ranches of Big Mama, the Supreme Pontiff heard the uproar of the monkeys agitated all night long by the passing of the crowds. On his nocturnal itinerary, the canoe had been filled with bags of yucca, stalks of green bananas, and crates of chickens, and with men and women who abandoned their customary pursuits to try their luck at selling things at Big Mama's funeral. His Holiness suffered that night, for the first time in the history of the Church, from the fever of insomnia and the torment of the mosquitoes. But the marvelous dawn over the Great Old Woman's domains, the primeval vision of the balsam apple and the iguana, erased from his memory the suffering of his trip and compensated him for his sacrifice.

Nicanor had been awakened by three knocks at the door which announced the imminent arrival of His Holiness. Death had taken possession of the house. Inspired by successive and urgent Presidential addresses, by the feverish controversies which had been silenced but continued to be heard by means of conventional symbols, men and congregations the world over dropped everything and with their presence filled the dark hallways, the jammed passageways, the stifling attics; and those who arrived later climbed up on the low walls around the church, the palisades, vantage points, timberwork, and parapets, where they accommodated themselves as best they could. In the central hall, Big Mama's cadaver lay mummifying while it waited for the momentous decisions contained in a quivering mound of telegrams. Weakened by their weeping, the nine nephews sat the wake beside the body in an ecstasy of reciprocal surveillance.

And still the universe was to prolong the waiting for many more days. In the city-council hall, fitted out with four leather stools, a jug of purified water, and a burdock hammock, the Supreme Pontiff suffered from a perspiring insomnia, diverting himself by reading memorials and administrative orders in the lengthy, stifling nights. During the day, he distributed Italian candy to the children who approached to see him through the window, and lunched beneath the hibiscus arbor with Father Anthony Isabel, and occasionally with Nicanor. Thus he lived for interminable weeks and months which were protracted by the waiting and the heat, until the day Father Pastrana appeared with his drummer in the middle of the plaza and read the proclamation of the decision. It was declared that Public Order was disturbed, ratatatat, and that the President of the Republic, ratatatat, had in his power the extraordinary prerogatives, ratatatat, which permitted him to attend Big Mama's funeral, ratatatat, tatatat, tatat, tatat.

The great day had arrived. In the streets crowded with carts, hawkers of fried foods, and lottery stalls, and men with snakes wrapped around their necks who peddled a balm which would definitively cure erysipelas and guarantee eternal life; in the mottled little plaza where the crowds had set up their tents and unrolled their sleeping mats, dapper archers cleared the Authorities' way. There they were, awaiting the supreme moment: the washerwomen of San Jorge, the pearl fishers from Cabo de la Vela, the fishermen from Ciénaga, the shrimp fishermen from Tasajera, the sorcerers from Mojajana, the salt miners from Manaure, the accordionists from Valledupar, the fine horsemen of Ayapel, the ragtag musicians from San Pelayo, the cock breeders from La Cueva, the improvisers from Sábanas de Bolívar, the dandies from Rebolo, the oarsmen of the Magdalena, the shysters from Monpox, in addition to those enumerated at the beginning of this chronicle, and many others. Even the veterans of Colonel Aureliano Buendía's camp—the Duke of Marlborough at their head, with the pomp of his furs and tiger's claws and teeth—overcame their centenarian hatred of Big Mama and those of her line and came to the funeral to ask the President of the Republic for the payment of their veterans' pensions which they had been waiting for for sixty years.

A little before eleven the delirious crowd which was sweltering in the sun, held back by an imperturbable élite force of warriors decked out in embellished jackets and filigreed morions, emitted a powerful roar of jubilation. Dignified, solemn in their cutaways and top hats, the President of the Republic and his Ministers, the delegations from Parliament, the Supreme Court, the Council of State, the traditional parties and the clergy, and representatives of Banking, Commerce, and Industry made their appearance around the corner of the telegraph office. Bald and chubby, the old and ailing President of the Republic paraded before the astonished eyes of the crowds who had seen him inaugurated without knowing who he was and who only now could give a true account of his existence. Among the archbishops enfeebled by the gravity of their ministry, and the military men with robust chests armored with medals, the Leader of the Nation exuded the unmistakable air of power.

In the second rank, in a serene array of mourning crêpe, paraded the national queens of all things that have been or ever will be. Stripped of their earthly splendor for the first time, they marched by, preceded by the universal queen: the soybean queen, the green-squash queen, the banana queen, the meal yucca queen, the guava queen, the coconut queen, the kidney-bean queen, the 255-mile-long-string-of-iguana-eggs queen, and all the others who are omitted so as not to make this account interminable.

In her coffin draped in purple, separated from reality by eight copper turnbuckles, Big Mama was at that moment too absorbed in her formaldehyde eternity to realize the magnitude of her grandeur. All the splendor which she had dreamed of on the balcony of her house during her heat-induced insomnia was fulfilled by those forty-eight glorious hours during which all the symbols of the age paid homage to her memory. The

Supreme Pontiff himself, whom she in her delirium imagined floating above the gardens of the Vatican in a resplendent carriage, conquered the heat with a plaited palm fan, and honored with his Supreme Dignity the greatest funeral in the world.

Dazzled by the show of power, the common people did not discern the covetous bustling which occurred on the rooftree of the house when agreement was imposed on the town grandees' wrangling and the catafalque was taken into the street on the shoulders of the grandest of them all. No one saw the vigilant shadow of the buzzards which followed the cortege through the sweltering little streets of Macondo, nor did they notice that as the grandees passed they left a pestilential train of garbage in the street. No one noticed that the nephews, godchildren, servants, and protégés of Big Mama closed the doors as soon as the body was taken out, and dismantled the doors, pulled the nails out of the planks, and dug up the foundations to divide up the house. The only thing which was not missed by anyone amid the noise of that funeral was the thunderous sigh of relief which the crowd let loose when fourteen days of supplications, exaltations, and dithyrambs were over, and the tomb was sealed with a lead plinth. Some of those present were sufficiently aware as to understand that they were witnessing the birth of a new era. Now the Supreme Pontiff could ascend to Heaven in body and soul, his mission on earth fulfilled, and the President of the Republic could sit down and govern according to his good judgment, and the queens of all things that have been or ever will be could marry and be happy and conceive and give birth to many sons, and the common people could set up their tents where they damn well pleased in the limitless domains of Big Mama, because the only one who could oppose them and had sufficient power to do so had begun to rot beneath a lead plinth. The only thing left then was for someone to lean a stool against the doorway to tell this story, lesson and example for future generations, so that not one of the world's disbelievers would be left who did not know the story of Big Mama, because tomorrow, Wednesday, the garbage men will come and will sweep up the garbage from her funeral, forever and ever.